FIND YOU AGAIN

BOOKS BY JAN THOMPSON

CITY/COASTAL/BEACH ROMANCE

Seaside Chapel (7 Books)

JanThompson.com/seaside

Savannah Sweethearts (12 Books)

JanThompson.com/savannah

Vacation Sweethearts (8 Books)

JanThompson.com/vacation

ROMANTIC SUSPENSE/THRILLERS

Protector Sweethearts (6 Books)

JanThompson.com/protector

Defender Sweethearts (6 Books)

JanThompson.com/defender

Binary Hackers (4 Books)

JanThompson.com/binary

JanThompson.com/books

FIND YOU AGAIN

SAVANNAH SWEETHEARTS
BOOK NINE

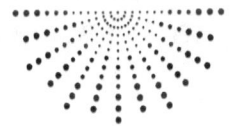

JAN THOMPSON

GEORGIA
PRESS

FIND YOU AGAIN (SAVANNAH
SWEETHEARTS BOOK 9)

To my Lord and Savior, Jesus Christ, who died on the cross to save me from my sins and rose again from the grave to give me eternal life in heaven.

For God so loved the world that He gave His only begotten Son, that whoever believes in Him should not perish but have everlasting life.
—John 3:16

READ A FREE EBOOK IN THE SAME STORY WORLD

Set in Georgia, South Carolina, and Tennessee, this clean and wholesome Christian romance tells the story of art gallery archivist Sheryl Breckenridge and world-famous sculptor Winton Pace. Read this ebook for free!

Time for Me (A Vacation Sweethearts Prequel)
JanThompson.com/time-free

ABOUT THE SAVANNAH SWEETHEARTS SERIES

Welcome to the new south! From *USA Today* bestselling author Jan Thompson come these clean and wholesome, sweet and inspirational Christian romances set in the coastal city of Savannah, Georgia, and on the beaches of Tybee Island by the Atlantic Ocean.

Meet a group of multiracial and multiethnic churchgoing Christians who love the Lord, work hard in their careers, and seek God's will for their love lives. Against a backdrop of ocean, sand, and sun, these inspirational romances showcase aspects of the human need for God and for one another.

Have some tea, settle in a comfortable reading chair, and enjoy these sweet celebrations of faith, hope, and love in Jesus Christ.

SAVANNAH SWEETHEARTS

- Book 1: Ask You Later
- Book 2: Know You More
- Book 3: Tell You Soon
- Book 4: Draw You Near
- Book 5: Cherish You So
- Book 6: Walk You There
- Book 7: Love You Always
- Book 8: Kiss You Now
- Book 9: Find You Again
- Book 10: Wish You Joy
- Book 11: Call You Home
- Book 12: Let You Go

While Savannah Sweethearts books can be read as standalone stories, you can see a bigger picture of the Riverside Chapel community and get a glimpse of the futures of previous characters if you read Books 1-12 in order.

Savannah Sweethearts:
JanThompson.com/sweethearts

For book news, sign up for Jan's mailing list:
JanThompson.com/newsletter

ABOUT FIND YOU AGAIN

SAVANNAH SWEETHEARTS BOOK 9

His flame for love died long ago...
She comes along and ignites a spark...
Will the fire last?

Firefighter Cheyenne Endecott appreciates bachelor Dr. Roger Patel for helping her widowed aunt settle into an assisted living resort. When Roger needs help dealing with a family problem, Cheyenne stands by him. One thing leads to another, and Roger starts having second thoughts about his bachelorhood and his friendship with Cheyenne in this friends-to-more romance novel.

ROGER'S RESOLUTIONS...

Having been burned too many times by former girl-friends, bachelor Roger Patel does not want a new relationship.

But there she is.

Set up by a mutual friend for a not-so-blind date, Roger goes to dinner with Cheyenne Endecott, not expecting anything more than to share a meal and celebrate their platonic friendship.

He is surprised by how much he enjoys spending time with Cheyenne.

Seriously, there's nothing going on between him and Cheyenne.

Or is there?

CHEYENNE'S CHOICES...

Grateful to God that Roger Patel has helped her widowed aunt find a trustworthy assisted living facility to spend the rest of her life on earth, fire-fighter Cheyenne Endecott does not want to jeopardize her friendship with Roger.

Still, what can come out of a simple dinner with a friend?

Besides, one casual dinner does not a romance make.

After all, Cheyenne has determined in her heart that she wants a godly Christian man for a husband, someone with proven integrity and a blameless testimony.

Well, someone like Roger—and yet not him.

No, it can't be him.

But there he is.

When Roger's past brings them together unexpectedly, Cheyenne finds herself spending more and more time in Roger's world, wondering what could happen and what might be...

DECISIONS, DECISIONS...

Roger needs a trustworthy confidant to help him deal with a skeleton in his family closet, and Cheyenne is more than happy to pray for him and do what she can. She feels that she is returning a favor.

One thing leads to another, and the favor starts to affect their friendship. Pretty soon, bachelor Roger is reconsidering his self-imposed moratorium on dating and relationships...

A multiracial romance between a bachelor and a firefighter, *Find You Again* is Book 9 in *USA Today* bestselling author Jan Thompson's Savannah Sweethearts series of clean and wholesome contemporary Christian romances set in the historic southern coastal city of Savannah, Georgia, and on the nearby idyllic Tybee Island by the Atlantic Ocean.

Find You Again (Savannah Sweethearts Book 9): JanThompson.com/find

FIND YOU AGAIN

PROLOGUE

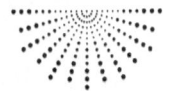

*A*fter buying three pounds of smoked Gouda cheese to take home to Savannah, Roger Patel wandered through the Schiphol Amsterdam Airport looking for a charging station for his dying phone.

That was when he saw her at the waiting area of one of the gates.

A woman in her thirties, maybe? Or older. Or younger.

Roger had always been bad with estimating ages when it came to women, especially one wearing a wool cap and a pair of thick glasses.

She was sleeping on a row of seats, one hand clutching a phone across her chest, an olive green US Army duffel bag at her feet on the seat at the end of the row.

Well, she might not be Army, but those laced-up boots made Roger wonder.

What he knew right now was that the woman's phone was about to slip out of her hand.

Ah, speaking of phones...

He had to recharge his own phone. That was why he was wandering up and down the airport, from gate to gate, looking for an outlet or a charging station.

Roger's eyes scanned up and down the rows of seats. Some were occupied, some didn't have charging stations, some had charging stations that were occupied.

One row down, Roger spotted an unused outlet with an empty seat.

This wasn't his gate, but he had a few more hours to spare before he boarded his flight to Atlanta. In Atlanta, he would rent a car and drive home to Savannah. It would take less than an hour to fly to the Georgia coast, but a car ride through the countryside would give him time alone with God to pray and evaluate his life.

He wasn't sure what he could evaluate, to be honest. He was happy with his job as the director of the Savannah Senior Living Resort on Tybee Island. He had paid off his mortgages. He lived alone without any dependents.

All in all, he had a peaceful, quiet life.

The calm before a storm?

Roger shrugged off the thought as he made a beeline for the charging station, when out of the corner of his eye, he spotted two men with backpacks approaching the sleeping woman.

The airport was crowded with travelers from all over the world.

But the men didn't walk past the woman. They walked toward the woman, and were now standing in front of her duffel bag at the woman's feet.

Roger stopped in his tracks.

And watched.

The men said nothing to each other.

Maybe they didn't want to wake the woman...

The men's expressionless faces put Roger on a Big Brother alert and he didn't know what to do. Memories of attending high school flooded his mind. So he instinctively did what he had done years ago to protect the girl he liked from school bullies.

He stepped in.

Nonchalantly, he walked toward the sleeping woman, said "excuse me" to the men, and lifted the duffel bag off the seat.

Yikes! What's in here? Bricks?

With great effort, he placed it on the floor.

Then Roger sat down in that seat and looked at the two men directly.

Quietly, they walked away.

As soon as they were out of sight, Roger winced, massaged his poor arm, and stood up.

He tried to put the duffel bag back on the seat.

"You can sit there."

Roger stopped moving the pile of rocks. He looked her way.

"The seat's not taken," the woman added.

"Well, this is not my gate," Roger explained. "I was looking for an outlet to charge my phone, when I saw..."

"Thank you."

Roger glanced at the screens above the doors. The flight was going to Dallas.

"I think the carry-on limit is fifteen pounds per bag," he said.

"Who's checking?" The woman chuckled.

She was still in that prone position. Between her big brown eyes and Roger's unending curiosity about the opposite genre—his bachelorhood notwithstanding—were those lug-sole army boots, that could possibly kick him all the way to the other end of the earth.

"I won't file any complaints." Roger lifted both palms.

"But..." Her eyes met his. "You want to know what's in my bag."

"None of my business."

"Books," she volunteered.

"Paperbacks or hardcovers?"

"Hardcovers."

Ah, my type of reader.

Roger adjusted his crossbody messenger bag, and lifted the flap. He pulled out a hardcover novel and showed it to the woman.

"Only one book?" She pointed to where the bookmark is. "Almost finished."

"I have hundreds of books on my iPad, but I usually sleep onboard. I get motion sickness when I look at a screen in flight."

"You too?" She sat up.

Her entire outfit was mismatched. Some sort of crazy-quilt jacket under an old fuzzy scarf.

Those Army boots, though...

What is her story?

Dare I ask?

Roger was curious about how this woman ended up here at the same airport as he was. They were both going home to the United States, though to different cities.

Should he ask?

Back at SSLR, he knew all about his residents. He knew where they had come from, why they were there, what their hopes and wishes were.

Even as far back as high school and college, Roger had always been curious about people. That curiosity followed him to medical school and then to those years of residency at Savannah Memorial Hospital, until he was invited to manage the then-new SSLR.

He has been at SSLR ever since.

It had been fifteen years now.

And yet, his curiosity about people had not waned. In fact, it had helped him with the residents because he knew all about their families.

But here was a total stranger...

He stared at her boots.

Again.

"What else do you want to know?" The woman put away her phone.

"Are you in the service?" Roger asked.

She nodded. "But there was no time to change into civilian clothes."

"No time?" Roger wondered what could possibly have been urgent.

"I'm here on a friendly military exercise—it's in the papers, so it's no secret—when I got a call that my uncle passed away in his sleep sometime this morning. My aunt freaked out, ran out of the bedroom, tripped, fell, and broke her hips. I'm her only living relative."

"Oh, I'm sorry." Roger wondered how he could help.

"Thanks. They gave me two weeks to deal with

6

the funeral. My uncle was a Marine, so the military is helping with the funeral and burial. But my aunt... I guess she has to go to a nursing home ASAP. I still have one year left to serve. I probably won't reenlist after that. I'm all Aunt Gemma has."

"I'm sorry."

"Don't be. This is life, you know."

"Still..."

"God is still good."

"All the time," Roger said, just as the announcement came that first class passengers could board.

Suddenly, he had an idea.

"Thank you for your service," he said.

"Glad to serve my God and my country," she said.

"What is your name?" Roger asked.

"Cheyenne Endecott. Yours?"

"Roger Patel. Let me do this for you. You flying economy?"

"Yeah. Why?"

"Let me buy you a business class ticket."

Cheyenne shook her head. "Oh, there's no need. No need."

"I want to. It's going to be difficult when you get home. You have jet lag and you need to be a caregiver. I know all about caregiving. So let me upgrade you to business class in honor of your uncle's service to our country."

Cheyenne blinked at the word *uncle.*

Tears pooled in her eyes.

"You have your ticket? Let's go." Roger tried to carry her duffel for her.

She waved him off. She lifted the bag easily.

Wow.

Suddenly Roger was impressed.

They waited in line to get to the counter.

Cheyenne was silent.

Roger wasn't sure what was in her mind. He felt that he had to say something. But she was probably grieving.

He had seen grief at SSLR. He had attended too many funerals there.

The Savannah Senior Living Resort might be on an oceanfront property with twenty-four-hour nurse care for the elderly, but it was the last place most of his residents went in their long and illustrious lives.

Last year alone, Roger had attended five funerals.

The pain, the grief, the memories were all intense.

As they inched toward the counter, Roger opened his wallet. He handed Cheyenne his business card.

"I didn't tell you that I work at an assisted living senior home," he said.

"Really?" Cheyenne seemed to be reading the

business card. "Says here you're Dr. Roger Patel. Like PhD or medical?"

"Medical, but I don't practice anymore. I've been only in administration for years."

"Savannah Senior Living Resort," Cheyenne continued reading.

"It's non-profit. We are affiliated with area churches and ministries that provide scholarships for veterans and widows of veterans. If your aunt needs a place to stay, maybe you could apply for a scholarship."

"Wow. That's a great idea. I need to look into it. Uncle Rupert earned a Purple Heart in Vietnam."

"Definitely something that the scholarship committee will take into consideration." Roger didn't want her to think it was an easy pass or a fast track for veterans to get end-of-life care. "I have to warn you that there's a waiting list."

"I understand."

"Shop around and compare all the facilities and centers around the country available for seniors, but you won't find a better one than ours. You can google and see what magazines and newspapers say about it. We have all sorts of residents—those who want a resort to frolic in, and those who need a lot of help."

"It says *resort*. It's not a nursing home?"

"No. We have an oceanfront row of condos and

villas that we rent out to able-bodied seniors. That helps us fund our assisted living facility. Sometimes we help the local hospital with their geriatric research, and we get extra funding that way. Otherwise we operate on charity."

"That's interesting. I've never heard of such a place."

"Neither had I until I started working there." Roger watched Cheyenne unzip her duffel bag and drop his business card into it.

He wondered if his business card would be lost in the stacks of books.

"Thank you for the information," Cheyenne said. "I hope to be able to take care of my aunt myself, but certainly, an assisted living facility is something we could consider."

Roger nodded. "Such a place can be expensive, yes, but scholarships can help."

"Why, though?"

"Why what?" Roger asked as they reached the front of the line. The staff behind the counter was busy typing.

"Why are you helping me?" Cheyenne asked, as the staffer motioned for them to approach her.

Roger shrugged. "I'm a Christian, and the Bible says that if it's within my means to help someone, I should."

"I'm a Christian too," Cheyenne said. "And I

will pray for God to bless you a millionfold for helping us."

"You protect our country and keep us all safe day after day. This is nothing."

Well, it wasn't *nothing* anymore when the airline staff told Roger that the entire business class was full, but would he like a first class upgrade instead?

First class?

Uh-oh.

Roger barely nodded as he slid his credit card across the counter.

CHAPTER ONE

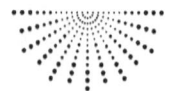

$\mathcal{M}$ ore than three years later, Roger Patel repeatedly regretted giving Cheyenne Endecott his business card.

As things had turned out, Cheyenne had moved her widowed aunt from one facility to another for one long year, until she caved in and applied for a scholarship for Miss Gemma Endecott to come to the wonderful coast of Georgia, to the land of flowers and koi fish.

And miracle of miracles, the Savannah Senior Living Resort scholarship committee approved Miss Gemma on her first try.

Because she was the wife of a highly decorated Vietnam War veteran, who had earned a Purple Heart saving an entire platoon of American soldiers from napalm bombs.

Because she had been sweeter than honey in the video interview.

Because she was Miss Gemma, after all.

Yes, Miss Gemma, also known as Mrs. Endecott, was source of many of Roger's consternations at SSLR, the ministry that loved to minister to the very needy.

Miss Gemma. Miss Gemma.

That's so British, isn't it?

A little echo all the way back to the old days of British rule centuries ago, when students called all their female teachers Miss, regardless of their marital status.

Well, that's what she wants to be called.

Even though Miss Gemma had retired from being a schoolteacher a long time ago, the teaching spirit still hadn't left her, especially when it came to teaching Roger, her favorite *student*.

It was too early in the morning for him to fuss about his residents, but as Roger got out of his car and walked into his SSLR office building, he glanced to the left and right to make sure he didn't see Miss Gemma anywhere.

Bless her heart.

Roger knew that Miss Gemma was only trying her best to live the rest of her life in harmony with God's plan.

But.

Accident prone, loud, and extremely nosy, Miss Gemma had been trying to tell him what to do at and with SSLR for the last two years. According to her, there was always something out of order with the place.

The koi pond was too small. She wanted more fish food.

The greenhouse didn't have enough ferns from Papua New Guinea.

The weather was too hot and humid in Georgia. She was homesick.

And worst of all, Miss Gemma had been trying to fix up Roger with her niece.

Whenever Roger said no, she would say, "Are you prejudiced against women firefighters?"

Well, Cheyenne hadn't always been a firefighter. When she had finished her commitment to the US Army, she was honorably discharged as a lieutenant. Instead of going into the reserves, Cheyenne had chosen to stay close to her aunt.

It was remarkable to Roger that Cheyenne had become a firefighter. He had nothing against firefighters, contrary to Miss Gemma's provocative remarks.

Of course not!

However, at the back of his mind, Roger doubted that Cheyenne, thirty, would date him, forty.

Their ten-year age difference seemed to be a gulf between cassettes and CDs, between paper and tablets.

Besides, Cheyenne was athletic, exercised a lot, and looked amazing. There was that glow on her face all the time, for some reason. And when she smiled...

Her smiles could knock out Roger's knees.

Ahem.

As for Roger, he had let his gym membership lapse—you know, as a matter of stewardship of money. Wasting money was a sin. If he was too busy to get to the gym, he shouldn't be paying for membership there, right?

Speaking of which, he wondered if they sold Spanx for men.

Roger pressed his belly a little as he checked the buttons on his wrinkle-free oxford shirt. All the buttons were intact.

But, yes, I need to exercise.

Next week, maybe.

He had two meetings today, another one tomorrow, and then a lot of staff planning meetings to decide how to expand SSLR.

The property next door had now become available. The owner would sell, but not for charity. In other words, they wanted too much money for it.

Before Roger could reach his office door, his phone buzzed.

Another text message.

Too early!

He glanced at his watch. It was only 6:50 a.m.

He decided not to check the message—

But it could be something important.

Against his better judgement, he peeked at his phone.

CHAPTER TWO

"She would want you to know that she doesn't like to eat alone," Owen said on the phone.

Roger didn't know when Owen the firefighter became Owen the big brother.

As far as he knew, Owen had been at the fire station longer than Cheyenne. He had taken Cheyenne under his wings, as though she were his little sister, and had protected her from the advances of any single man, firefighter or not.

In effect, Owen helped Cheyenne filter out who she should not date.

Cheyenne was pretty popular in the single's group at Riverside Chapel—where Roger also attended—although her boyfriends and dates had not attended their church.

Roger supposed that made it easier for her to break up with them without having to see them again in the same church setting—

Why should I care?

Roger took a deep breath. He rocked in his executive chair. On the other side of his oak desk, the two seats were empty, and beyond that, the door with a frosted panel was closed.

He shouldn't have responded to the text message, which had led Owen to know that he was awake.

He shouldn't have answered the call, which had come seconds after he had texted Owen back.

"She wants you to know," Owen repeated.

"Is that so? She told you to call me?" Roger asked.

"Look, you know I'm watching out for her."

"She didn't tell you to call me." That much, Roger knew about Cheyenne. "Lying is a sin, Owen. You knew that."

Ever since they had met again about two and a half years ago, Cheyenne had frequented SSLR almost every week to visit her aunt.

Sometimes the local fire department visited at Christmas to sing carols to the residents. Sometimes they raised funds to bring cheer to the residents.

All in all, Roger had crossed paths with

Cheyenne quite frequently, and they had developed a platonic friendship with each other.

Roger had even given Cheyenne the direct line to his office, in case she needed to call him about Miss Gemma.

Through Cheyenne and the charity activities, Roger had come to know the other members of the local fire station, especially Owen, who was about Cheyenne's age.

"Why don't you take her out?" Roger asked suddenly.

"That would be awkward."

"Awkward how?"

"She and I work together. We even do the same shifts together. People will talk."

"So people won't talk if I take her out?"

"Technically, you're not taking her out. She's going to be eating alone tonight at Piper's Place at eight o'clock. Tonight. Tuesday."

"I know what day this is."

"She will be already sitting there."

"So? I eat alone all the time."

"Exactly, Roger. So I'm trying to help both of you."

"I don't need any help. I'm a happy bachelor." His last girlfriend had been over a year ago.

Since that breakup, he had plunged into work at

SSLR. To be sure, there was a lot of work to do, even though he now had an assistant director.

"I say that too, but somewhere in my heart, I know someone special will come along," Owen said.

"Good for you. I guess you didn't hear me right. I am happy alone."

"Yeah, Cheyenne's going to be alone tonight. She just broke up with her boyfriend of three months. She's miserable and all that. So we've been trying to get her to go out, and she finally decided to humor us. But you see what she's doing? She's going out alone!"

"Well, maybe she wants to be alone," Roger suggested.

"You think she likes to be by herself?"

"I don't know, Owen. It's not my problem, is it?"

"No, but don't Christians help one another?"

"Don't play that card, or you're going to have to repent again," Roger said.

"Play what card?"

"The Christian card."

"In what way?"

Roger didn't feel like debating. The last time he had done this, it cost him a hundred dollars paying for Cheyenne's dinner.

Yes, he had gone out with her before. Exactly seven months ago, when she had broken up with another barely-boyfriend.

Funny how it went. Cheyenne had told Roger on their dinner out that night, that she was looking for a man of God.

Then she had gone to date another sorry loser—

Roger stopped himself, remembering the verse he had been teaching in Sunday School at Riverside Chapel. John 8:7 ran though his mind now.

So when they continued asking Him, He raised Himself up and said to them, "He who is without sin among you, let him throw a stone at her first."

Roger swallowed.

I'm not worthy of Cheyenne, and I will never be.

CHAPTER THREE

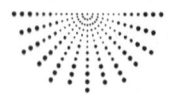

Cheyenne Endecott was reading an ebook on her phone at a corner booth on the third floor of Piper's Place, when she heard someone call her name.

She wished she could put a sign at her table saying, "Do not disturb!"

But this wasn't her restaurant.

She kept reading.

"I know you can hear me." The male voice was quiet, but unmistakable.

There was only one person with that voice.

Roger Patel.

He had called her name as he drew close, so as not to startle her. But right now, right here, he was trying to make light of the whole thing.

Cheyenne didn't look up. "I know who put you up to it."

"I won't make you pay for my dinner," Roger said. "But at least invite me to sit down, or I'll have to find my own miserable, lonely book."

"All right. Sit." Cheyenne put down her phone on the table.

As Roger made himself comfortable across the table, he pointed to her phone. "Whatcha reading?"

"How to get rid of men in two words." Cheyenne laughed.

"What? 'Go away!' doesn't work anymore?" Roger frowned.

A server came to their table before Cheyenne could respond.

Cheyenne was a bit surprised at Roger's reaction to the server. She was about eighteen or nineteen, with big brown eyes.

Cheyenne didn't see a name tag. "What's your name?"

"Leila," the server said. She didn't give her last name.

Her accent was somewhat midwestern, but Cheyenne couldn't place her origins. She looked like she was biracial. Maybe.

After she left, Cheyenne turned her attention to Roger, wondering whose neck she had to wring. "Tell me who told you that I'm here."

"You know. Your self-appointed big brother."

"Why, though?"

Roger leaned back against the backrest of his bench. "You say, 'Why, though?' a lot, don't you?"

"What do you mean?"

"Do you remember the first time we ever met?"

Cheyenne smiled. "That was providential, wasn't it? I was at the end of my rope. I had six months left in my commitment to the Army, but with my uncle dead, someone had to take care of Aunt Gemma. Sending her through several assisted living homes in six months was a torture. And then another six months of moving with her from town to town..."

"But you kept my business card all that time," Roger said. "You could have thrown it out."

"I thought about doing that, to be honest, but you must be a real Samaritan if you paid for my first class ticket that day." She still remembered their encounter vividly even though it had been more than three years. "After you heroically rescued me from those two pickpockets."

"You were fast asleep."

"Actually, I'm a light sleeper. And I knew they had approached me."

"If I hadn't been there there..."

"I would've kicked them where it hurt the most with my army boots."

"Ouch," Roger said as his sweet tea arrived. He sprinkled more sugar into it. "Remind me never to get on your dark side."

"I don't have a dark side," Cheyenne protested. "Christ in me is my eternal light."

"True, but we do all have good days and bad."

Cheyenne had to agree with that. Right now she wasn't feeling too great. Owen had probably told Roger all about her failed relationships.

"Why are you here, Roger?" Cheyenne asked.

"It's not because Owen made me do it." Roger didn't laugh. "It's not because I feel sorry for both of us. It's because we're friends, and we're eating alone tonight."

"Okay. So Owen made you do it."

"I just said he didn't."

"Then you refuted yourself by saying we're two lonely people in the world tonight."

"Not anymore, are we? Not right now, anyway." Roger grinned.

"And we can't say this is technically a date night, since we came separately, and would have eaten at separate tables."

"Right. And we'll pay separately, unless you don't mind me picking up the tab."

"Ah, no need. I'm still paying off that first class ticket from three years ago."

"Well..."

Cheyenne shook her head. "If you ever need a favor someday..."

"I told you that was a gift. Don't try to pay me back."

"Makes me feel bad that you wanted to pay for a business class upgrade, but it ended up costing you twice as much."

Roger shrugged. "Well, if you want to do something for me, you can help me manage your aunt."

"Aunt Gemma?" Cheyenne's eyes widened. "What has she done now?"

"She thinks we need to have a second pond and fill it with goldfish."

Cheyenne chuckled. "Koi not enough for her?"

"I've already approved an entire section of the garden for her millions of daffodils."

Cheyenne felt touched. "Thank you for that. It means a lot to her, since she can't go to Atlanta to see her daffodils at the botanical gardens there."

Roger nodded. "It's not a big deal. The thing is, I see her every single day."

"Some day, she won't be here anymore..."

Roger's eyes widened again. "Cheyenne, I'm sorry."

Cheyenne tried to hold it in. She looked away, out of the third-floor window and across River Street, toward the dark skies over the Savannah River.

Some day, Aunt Gemma will be gone, just like Uncle Rupert.

While Cheyenne's consolation was that both of them would be in heaven, she also knew that earth would be a lonely place for her the rest of her life.

Her aunt was her only relative.

"Cheyenne." Roger reached across the table. He seemed to hesitate, but then he placed his entire palm on top of Cheyenne's hand. "Look, I was halfway joking about your aunt. There are two hundred residents to manage at SSLR. I get over-whelmed sometimes."

Cheyenne nodded, distracted.

His hand felt warm.

Warm and cozy.

Cheyenne didn't know whether that was good or bad. They were friends, so it must not be bad. They were truly platonic friends who went to the same church.

But more than that, they had one thing in common: both had to deal with Aunt Gemma.

And both of them were very lonely people.

Maybe two of the loneliest people in the whole wide world.

CHAPTER FOUR

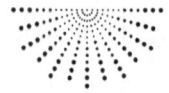

"Cheyenne," Roger said again. "I'm sorry."

"You said that." Cheyenne pulled her hand away. She clasped her two hands together on her lap under the table.

"I'm happy that Miss Gemma is at SSLR. She's the sunshine of the place when there's a big thunderstorm outside."

"She's why I was able to live and continue living, when my own single mom abandoned me at her doorstep twenty-five years ago. She took me in, fed me, clothed me, and sent me to school. Never complained."

"So I want to be nice to her," Roger said. "That's what I meant. But I don't know how to deal with her. Maybe you can help me."

"It's been a little more than two years since she's

been at SSLR. Why are you bringing her up at this time?"

"Well, maybe because she and I are both older now, and we have quirks. We seem to be irritating each other every day," Roger said. "Also, I thought if we talked about your aunt, it might take your mind off your breakup."

Cheyenne's jaw dropped. "I don't understand you, Roger."

"Well, sometimes I don't understand myself."

"I wouldn't say you're eccentric. Might you be a little selfish?" Cheyenne blurted.

She heard a gasp, looked to her left, and found their server staring at Roger, the tray of food in her arms shaking.

Cheyenne wondered how much Leila had heard of their conversation. She had just called Roger self-ish, and the server had gasped. Were the two reactions connected?

"I—I'll be back to top off your tea," Leila said after she placed the right dishes in front of the right people.

The grilled catfish in front of Cheyenne smelled delicious. She looked across the table. "Wow. Fried chicken. Did you know that studies have shown that fried stuff could shorten your life?"

"You mean I'll go to heaven faster?" Roger struck back.

"I'm sorry. I'll shut up now. Eat up."

Cheyenne felt sorry for taking it out on Roger. Well, she had specifically told Owen not to play matchmaker anymore, and here he went again, inviting Roger into her one-person pity party.

It wasn't Roger's fault that her last two boyfriends had been a total disaster.

Well, one was Owen's obsessive cousin.

The other was Owen's old high school football friend.

Both had ended up in breakups. Truth be told, Cheyenne's standards were too high for them. They could never meet them.

She had prayed to God for a godly Christian man for a husband, someone with proven integrity and a blameless testimony.

That was the type of man she wanted to spend the rest of her life with.

Where is that sort of man, Lord?

Cheyenne watched Roger drink his sweet tea silently. She was about to tell him that all that sugar would settle in his already tight—not taut, but tight in his clothes—belly.

But she was not close enough to Roger to be that frank and honest with him.

Besides, it was his health, not hers.

"I know what you're thinking," Roger said.

"You do?" Cheyenne finished her last piece of

catfish. She realized she was selfish too, never offering any of it to Roger.

Well, she wanted to eat the whole piece herself, thank you very much.

It was her comfort food.

"You're thinking this sweet tea is the end of me," Roger continued.

"Not exactly."

"No? Then what were you thinking?"

Cheyenne shrugged. "Don't mind me. My thoughts are irrational right now. I'm not feeling too great, to be honest. I wanted to stay at home, but Owen said I needed to get out. He thinks I need to get back into my routine."

"You do have a routine at work."

"Yeah. But he meant that I need to get back to my normal life without a boyfriend."

Roger pushed away his plate, and wiped his hands on a cloth napkin. "At least your boyfriend left when you dumped him, right?"

"How did you know I left him?" Cheyenne folded her arms across her chest.

"He's probably not good enough for you."

"It might be prideful to say such a thing." Truly, Cheyenne wanted a man of God. So far, nobody had measured up. "Let's just say we're incompatible."

"Like how?" Roger asked.

JAN THOMPSON

"Must you ask? You've been nosy since day one. Remember when we were in Amsterdam? You wanted to know what was in my duffel bag."

Roger cringed. "Okay, okay. Don't tell me about your boyfriends. I don't need to know."

"Seriously, why are you curious, though?" Cheyenne asked.

"I'm curious about people. People are fascinating."

"Except my aunt? You want to avoid her like the plague." Cheyenne could not retract it. Well, she wasn't trying to please Roger or make friends. If she had to choose between Roger or Aunt Gemma, she would pick her own aunt. Of course.

"Your aunt, I don't understand." Roger picked up the dessert menu from the inside end of the booth table. "Nope. I don't understand her at all."

"Your cousin gets her," Cheyenne said.

"Pri?"

Cheyenne nodded. "Why not let Priyanka handle my aunt? She has better bedside manners than you do. And she can summarize for you what Aunt Gemma needs."

Roger stared at her.

"What?" Cheyenne stared back.

"You're brilliant."

"No, I'm not. You could have thought about that

32

idea yourself if you hadn't been so busy running away from my aunt."

Roger laughed. "She scares me. Lately, she's been lining up daughters and nieces for me to choose from."

"No kidding. I'd be scared too if she did that to me."

"Well, you *are* on her list."

"No way."

Roger looked hurt. "What do you mean by *no way*? Are you saying I'm off your radar?"

"Don't be silly. You were never on my radar in the first place."

And Cheyenne immediately regretted saying it.

CHAPTER FIVE

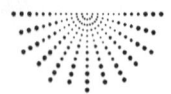

*V*isiting her aunt on her days off had been a routine for Cheyenne, and though she tried to do something different each time, Aunt Gemma only wanted to talk about the weather, her fish, and her daffodils.

This morning, in between lunch and nap time, while Aunt Gemma was still somewhat awake—none of her medication could keep her out of her pink wheelchair—they went strolling down the garden path of the newly planted "fields of daffodils," as Aunt Gemma described it.

All the other residents of the Savannah Senior Living Resort loved this new addition to the grounds, and had thanked Roger Patel for it.

"Oh, he's not one to brag, that Dr. Patel," Aunt Gemma explained. "He insisted that it was Priyanka's idea that Hunter had somehow gotten the head gardener to implement. But can I tell you a little secret?"

Cheyenne smiled as she pushed the quiet wheelchair. "What's the secret?"

Aunt Gemma looked to the left, and then to the right.

There were some other residents around them. Some were doing light exercises on the green grass of springtime on Tybee Island. Cheyenne doubted anyone was listening to their chat.

Aunt Gemma lifted a wobbly hand up to her mouth, and whispered rather loudly, "I think he likes the daffodils himself. Ask me why."

"Why, Aunt Gemma?"

"Because every time I see him walk this way, he smiles."

Cheyenne nodded as she surveyed the flower garden. There weren't only daffodils there, but also gladiolas and azaleas. Truth be told, she preferred azaleas herself, but all these flowers were beautiful.

"God made such pretty flowers, didn't He?" Cheyenne ask.

"Indeed." Aunt Gemma pointed to some Japanese maple trees here and there. "And trees too."

Truth be told, the sandy soil of Tybee Island had to be worked on to make all these flowers and trees grow on it. Cheyenne recalled the stories that Aunt Gemma had told her about the old days, when Savannah had been the thirteenth British colony, back when they could hardly grow anything on Tybee Island.

Now you could plant anything.

When it rained, Cheyenne and her aunt would stroll in the SSLR greenhouse, where tropical plants abound.

Today was unseasonably warm at the end of March. Well, it wasn't hot and humid, like summertime, but it also wasn't cold, like winter.

Cheyenne heard a sneeze.

A man's sneeze.

Normally, she wouldn't pay attention, but she knew whose sneeze that was.

It wasn't odd, in case anybody asked, that Cheyenne could recognize Roger's sneeze. They both attended the same church, sat in the same Sunday School, participated in numerous ministry projects over the last two years, and had frequent lunches—and even dinners—with each other and others.

They were no more than friends, since they preferred to date other people.

But friends, nonetheless.

Cheyenne would've ignored the sneeze, except

that Aunt Gemma had heard it too, and she was now making a fuss.

"Dr. Patel! Dr. Patel!" Aunt Gemma shouted at the top of her voice.

Suddenly a loud horn blared.

Cheyenne's hands immediately cupped her ears, and she shut her eyes as the horn continued.

"What in the world?" Roger's voice drew nearer, as did the sounds of soles on cement.

Cheyenne opened her eyes, afraid of what she might see.

Honk!

Cheyenne flinched.

Roger let out some sort of garbled words.

Aunt Gemma chuckled. She squeezed the bright-yellow bike horn again.

Honk! Honk!

"Where did you get that, Miss Gemma?" Roger asked calmly.

"I want to know too," Cheyenne said. "Where did you hide it? I didn't see it when we left your room."

"It's a Christmas present," Aunt Gemma said calmly, ignoring all their questions.

"But it's April," Cheyenne said.

"Christmas is almost here. Just ask Mrs. Untermeyer."

Roger rolled his eyes.

"Mrs. Untermeyer?" Cheyenne asked. "Did she give you the horn?"

"No, dear. I got it from someone else."

"Who?"

"I can't tell you. Her granddaughter will be mad that she doesn't want the present."

Roger cleared his throat. "We have rules here, Miss Gemma. That would be excessive noise."

"Tsk. Tsk. I could hardly hear it," Aunt Gemma said. "Even with my hearing aid."

Roger glanced at Cheyenne.

Cheyenne shrugged. She waited to see how Roger would handle Aunt Gemma.

She wondered how long she'd have to wait because Roger just stood there, stumped. All those years of medical school, all these years of running this retirement home, and he had nothing to say.

Cheyenne could step in.

Or not.

Let's wait and see.

Roger looked at her. His mouth started to open. Then it shut again.

Under the afternoon sunshine, Cheyenne could see crow's feet on both sides of Roger's eyes, and some more wrinkles on his forehead—appearing usually when he was concerned about something. His chin was clean-shaven. Cheyenne wondered if he had ever kept a mustache.

Honk!

Honk! Honk! Honk!

Instantly, Roger snatched that bike horn out of Aunt Gemma's hand, said not a word, and walked away from them.

Cheyenne realized then that there was something she didn't know about Roger. Could it be that when he couldn't handle something, he would leave the scene?

Wasn't that a normal thing to do, though?

It would be better not to be embroiled in a conflict he didn't know how to get out of, rather than to stay around to see what happened.

"He's rude!" Aunt Gemma snapped. "I want my horn back! I paid for it."

"Paid? You bought it?" Cheyenne asked, a thousand things going through her mind. "With what?"

"Money, what else?" Aunt Gemma brushed her off.

Cheyenne didn't remember giving her aunt any cash. At the SSLR, everything was paid for. If the residents needed something from the little on-side convenience store or extra midnight snacks, the costs would be added to their account.

To date, Aunt Gemma hadn't been a spender. She ate in the dining hall for all her meals, and she hardly asked for any snacks. In fact, Cheyenne had to bring chips and chocolate as surprises for Aunt Gemma.

And here she was owning a bike horn.

"I was going to ask Hunter to install it to my chair here," Aunt Gemma continued. "It could help with traffic flow."

"What traffic flow?"

Again, Aunt Gemma ignored her question. She patted her arm rest. "Right here."

"Where would you put your arm if you tied a bike horn to your armrest?" Cheyenne asked.

Aunt Gemma shrugged. "We won't find out now, will we? My horn has been confiscated."

"You heard Roger, Aunt Gemma. There's a noise rule around here. We don't want you to get demerits."

"We don't get demerits here, dear." Aunt Gemma laughed. Then her face fell. "I'm done with the daffodils. Please take me to my fish now."

"Yes, ma'am."

Cheyenne glanced at her watch. It was closing in on nap time. "After we feed the fish, we need to get you back to your room."

"And you will read the Bible to me."

"Yes, as I always do when I'm off work."

Aunt Gemma reached back over her shoulder and tried to pat Cheyenne's hand. "I thank God for you, Cheyenne."

"I thank God for you too, Aunt Gemma."

As they passed by benches and azaleas, Cheyenne spotted Roger at the greenhouse entrance, the yellow bike horn in his hand. He was talking to the head gardener.

Standing next to them was Hunter Jacobs. From what Aunt Gemma had told Cheyenne, Hunter was Roger's cousin's husband. Hunter had married Priyanka the year before.

As they reached the greenhouse, Aunt Gemma waved to Hunter, and he came over.

"How are we doing, Miss Gemma?" Hunter asked.

"I'll feel better when my niece gets herself a husband," Aunt Gemma said without batting an eyelid.

Cheyenne gasped.

"Did I ever tell you she's a firefighter?" Aunt Gemma reached for Hunter's hand.

Hunter nodded. "Yes. Firefighter. Compound word."

Cheyenne stood behind the wheelchair, feeling a bit awkward. Here was her dear aunt, talking about her lack of dating life.

Roger stepped toward them. "Miss Gemma, you can't have this bike horn because it's too loud."

"What did you say?" Aunt Gemma put dainty

fingers on her earlobes. "Can't hear you. Speak louder."

Roger looked at Cheyenne, still standing behind the wheelchair.

She put her hands up in the air. *Don't look at me.*

"I'm going to give this horn to your niece," Roger said. "She can keep it for you in *her* home. Not here at SSLR. Okay?"

"Well... Can I toot it one last time?" Aunt Gemma pleaded.

"Nope. Rules are rules." Roger stepped around the wheelchair.

After he handed the horn to Cheyenne, his hand reached above her head. When it came down, Cheyenne saw that he was holding a tiny drying leaf.

The wind must've blown it onto her hair when she and Aunt Gemma were in the garden.

"Sorry that it's not a flower." Roger handed it to her. "I'll do better next time."

And he walked away from them a second time today.

CHAPTER SIX

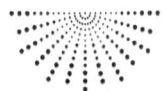

*E*very first Thursday afternoon of the month, SSLR hosted a tea time for its residents.

It was that glorious hour at SSLR, where almost every resident who was awake—or who couldn't nap due to their medication—showed up in the dining hall for their tea and biscuits.

Biscuits.

Cookies, actually.

Standing at the door, Roger's eyes were upon a cart of cookies passing by in front of him. On the tray were many types of cookies that the Super Seniors of Riverside Chapel had baked. That group of retirees and semi-retirees had been a blessing to SSLR.

"Want some?" The college student asked him.

"I better not. Dieting." Roger didn't know why that came out of his mouth. He wasn't dieting!

Well, he had to, regardless of whether he looked as buff as those male bodybuilder firefighters that Cheyenne worked with—

Why did I think this way?

A shrill voice called his name.

As if by reflex, Roger's hand reached for the door handle behind him. He was turning when something bumped into his legs.

Large wheels.

And a shoe.

He closed his eyes, tried to pray something.

No prayer popped into his head.

He took a deep breath and turned around. "Miss Gemma, how are you today?"

"Caught you just as you were leaving to visit my niece?" Miss Gemma's face was pink with delight.

Or she might have applied too much rose rouge —or something—on her cheekbones.

"Niece?" Roger mumbled.

"Cheyenne Endecott. My niece. My only niece. How many nieces do you think I have?" Miss Gemma tsk-tsked. She glanced at the nurse pushing her wheelchair. "He forgot her already."

"Cheyenne." Roger swallowed. "Uh... I haven't seen her since last week."

Miss Gemma waved her hot pink fingernails at him.

Roger Patel wondered if there was toxin in fingernail polish.

Wave, wave.

"She's probably waiting for you to call," Miss Gemma said.

"She's probably busy fighting fires," Roger retorted.

I have fires of my own.

Miss Gemma nodded. "I guess she is. She hasn't called me in four hours."

"Four hours? It's still daylight."

Miss Gemma looked at Roger with droopy eyelids and sagging eyebrows.

Roger had no idea how she could make herself look like a poor little puppy in need of a pick-me-up.

"Could you please call her and check on her?" Miss Gemma placed her clasped—and trembling—hands on her chest. "Make sure she's all right?"

Roger felt like crying.

The things he had to do to prove he did somehow have bedside manners tucked away some-where at the back of his medical resume.

Somewhere.

"Please?" Miss Gemma asked in some sort of weepy voice.

Roger had never felt more manipulated in his life.

I gave her a fish pond. I gave her a daffodil patch. I gave her a scholarship.

Roger flinched.

No. No. No. I got all that wrong, didn't I?

Roger stared at his watch, as if this was his timeout to think.

Lord Jesus, please forgive me for taking credits for what You have done.

"Are you holding your breath?" Miss Gemma asked suddenly.

"Huh? What?" Roger dropped his arm to his side. "What made you say that?"

"You were staring at your watch, and your face was turning red."

"I...uh... I was just looking at the time." It was partially true, but while staring at his watch, he had prayed and asked God to forgive him for his pride.

"Time to call my niece. Thank you. You're such a dear." Miss Gemma clapped her hands, and waved for her nurse to wheel her away.

"Wait a minute." Roger lifted his hand, just as his phone rang.

The musicians from Riverside Chapel began to play a song. Everyone cheered and sang along almost immediately.

Roger's phone kept ringing.

CHAPTER SEVEN

utside the dining hall, Roger could still hear the singing behind the door and wall. He could barely hear his phone.

"This is Roger Patel." He stuck the phone to one ear, while his other hand covered the other ear.

He decided to walk outside where most people weren't at this time.

Outside the glass doors, the smooth cement wheelchair path led toward the greenhouse and the wing where Pastor Hiram used to live until God called him home to heaven.

Roger still missed him from time to time, but not as much as his cousin and her husband did.

"Hello?" Roger tried again, hoping for a better reception.

He made a note to self to get more Wi-Fi coverage for the entire outdoor space. Of course, money had to be rationed toward the more important end-of-life matters, such as quality of living and care for these elderly souls.

To be honest, Roger was getting a bit weary of attending funerals.

He wished that people had lived longer, but at the same time, parting was always bittersweet, whether the residents were Christians or not.

One way or another, we all die.

Yet, we also live.

The paradox was nothing short of miraculous.

Roger made another mental note of adding that to his Sunday School lesson. Yes, he was still teaching that class at Riverside Chapel. And yes, he was still filling in for Diego—he still had a hard time calling his friend Pastor Flores—in the Sunday evening service whenever the pastor went out of town.

In more ways than he could ever count, Roger had never felt adequate about it.

He had enough sins in his life to make him unworthy of being a Sunday School teacher, let alone preach the Sunday evening sermon at church. To Diego's credit, he had never once asked Roger to preach the Sunday morning sermon, and neither had he suggested that Roger go to seminary.

All because of that one blight in his life.

One blight.

One blight to ruin them all.

"Hello?" Roger was talking to empty space.

Whoever had called was gone.

Maybe he had picked up the phone too late. Or something.

Roger stopped in his tracks. Looked up. Saw the Atlantic Ocean.

Whoa. How did I walk this far?

Well, the boardwalk wasn't that far from the main buildings of SSLR. In fact, to his left, the boardwalk extended toward the oceanfront villas that SSLR had rented out to help pay the bills.

Thanks to that bit of business and the generosity of private donations from everywhere, SSLR had been able to remain in the black ever since Roger became the director.

Roger dug into his pockets. No sunglasses.

He squinted in the afternoon sun. It was spring-time again, but it wasn't too warm yet. He looked for a bench to sit down and take a break.

Maybe take stock of his life.

Priyanka was an excellent assistant director. She was great with the residents. They all loved her. Even those who hated the place had come to accept that this was a better place for them than to live alone with no family around them. All because Priyanka loved them unconditionally.

Like Christ loves us.

His phone rang again. This time, Roger swiped to answer at the first ringtone. "Roger Patel."

"Mimi Mays."

Roger nearly dropped his phone into the sand beneath his loafers at the foot of the bench.

"Hello?" Mimi said.

Roger took a deep breath. "I'm here."

"You never thought I'd call again."

"No." The last time Roger had spoken with Mimi was five years ago, when he had sent her his final bank deposit.

Their whirlwind relationship had been over between them nineteen years ago.

However, three years after that, Mimi had tracked him down, shocked him with the news of a then two-year-old daughter, and made him send her money for the next eleven years.

At the end of the eleventh year, Roger finally swallowed his pride and hired his private investigator friend, Ming Wei, to look into the extortion. It had turned out that Mimi also told four other men that her daughter was theirs.

Somehow all five men had sent her their DNA reports, and they had all matched her daughter's. Who helped her fabricate the results?

Still, Roger knew that he would not get his money back.

Five years ago.

I thought it's over.

Why is she calling me now?

If he hadn't been so ashamed of what he had done back in medical school, he would have hired Ming sooner. On the other hand, Ming had just transitioned to his private investigator job at that time, so he might not have the know-how to track down the truth behind a chronic liar's schemes.

Then again, he would never know.

All water under the bridge.

Now it's flooding again.

"How did you get this number?" Roger asked.

"It's not that hard, according to my PI boyfriend."

"Boyfriend? What happened to your husband?" Roger really didn't want to chitchat, but he was a curious man.

A curious man?

I only meant that I'm curious.

Have a sub-conversation all by himself was a warning sign to him that he was about to face something huge, something beyond his own ability to handle...

"He's ancient history," Mimi said. "We

divorced, and I went on to marry twice more after him."

"And this boyfriend is not your husband." Roger remembered a passage in the New Testament about the woman at the well who slept around. John 4:18 could be another anchor verse for a Sunday School message in the future.

> ...for you have had five husbands, and the one whom you now have is not your husband; in that you spoke truly.

Roger didn't ask Mimi how many husbands she had—

And then another passage of Scripture popped into Roger's head, that one where the Lord Jesus Christ was teaching the townspeople a lesson about sin when an adulteress was brought to Him.

> So when they continued asking Him, He raised Himself up and said to them, "He who is without sin among you, let him throw a stone at her first."

John 8:7 was very clear. Roger felt a conviction in his heart about not condemning Mimi for the sins she had committed, not when everyone had sinned and fallen short of the glory of God.

When no one could cast the first stone at the adulterous woman, Jesus gave her a warning in John 8:11.

And Jesus said to her, "Neither do I condemn you; go and sin no more."

Roger thought he could outline a Sunday School lesson out of this. He made another mental note for himself.

"Are you still there?" Mimi's voice came across the phone.

And torched Roger's mental notes.

I can't teach that lesson.

His shoulders dropped and his spine sagged as he still sat there on the bench.

Heaven forbid he had to call upon his church home to help him through.

Only Diego and Ming knew.

Only his two best buddies.

No one else knew.

And definitely not Cheyenne.

Oh why, Lord? Why now? Why is Mimi calling me at this time when Cheyenne and I are finally warming up to each other?

Cheyenne?

This problem was bigger than Cheyenne.

"What do you want, Mimi?" Roger snapped, all his Christian politeness going out the window.

"Our daughter—"

"Let me stop you right there." Roger's hand went up in the wind, though Mimi couldn't see him. "According to my own PI, you sent five men some forged DNA results. I'm surprised no one has taken legal actions against you."

"One of the three of you out of five..."

Roger flinched again. "Don't even talk to me."

But he didn't hang up.

"She hasn't come home in two weeks." Mimi's voice sounded teary.

Yeah, like some people's voices when they wanted something.

"Two weeks?" Roger asked. "And you just found out?"

"I thought she went on a school trip."

"You thought?"

"She has one year left in high school, sure, but by all practical purposes, she's an adult. I don't keep track of an eighteen-year-old wayward girl when I've got four other little children to take care of."

"How many kids in total do you have—never mind. Call the police. Don't call me." Especially since the girl was probably not Roger's flesh and blood.

Or any of the five gullible men's, possibly.

"I found a note this morning when I was doing the wash," Mimi said.

After two weeks? How frequently do you do laundry anyway?

"She left me a note, Roger," Mimi repeated. "Are you sitting down?"

CHAPTER EIGHT

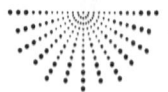

*C*heyenne thought it was brazen of the arsonists to call the local news media before they showed their handiwork in the middle of a Wednesday afternoon rush hour, in one of the busiest squares in downtown Savannah, where not only were historic homes at risk of being razed, but old live oak trees would also be burned up like firewood.

Surrounding fire stations from Pooler and Richmond had sent their firetrucks to support the Savannah firefighters. Cheyenne was thankful for that until the call came that yet another historic home—fifteen minutes away at the other side of town—was on fire.

The Pooler firefighters left to take care of that.

By the time Cheyenne, Owen, and the rest of

their team rolled away from the blackened early-twentieth-century hotel, everyone was too exhausted to say a single word.

And no one talked as they backed the firetruck into the fire station, where a hot dinner awaited them—after they put away their gear, and showered off the smoke and grime from their faces.

By the time Cheyenne sat down to eat, she had missed numerous text messages from her seemingly distraught Aunt Gemma.

Plus a few curt texts from Roger Patel.

Wait. Who?

Cheyenne chewed a piece of chicken slowly as she reread the text from Roger. It wasn't unfriendly. It wasn't in a familiar tone either. All Roger had tried to convey was that she should call her aunt as soon as possible before her aunt called 911.

Five hours ago.

Cheyenne composed a text—then deleted it.

She placed the phone down on the table, and wondered how much of Roger's short, unfeeling message had anything to do with what she had said to him Tuesday night.

You were never on my radar in the first place.

Rationalizing it, Cheyenne was sure that he would have forgotten about it by now. There was nothing between her and Roger.

In the last two years, they had lunches and

dinners occasionally. Platonic meals. Business meals. Most of the time there were other people around.

People like Owen across the table, looking at him.

"Everything all right?" he asked.

Owen, Owen.

He would make a wonderful husband, for sure. Sensitive, caring—albeit often in-your-face.

Like now.

"Yes, fine," Cheyenne answered.

"Something you saw on your phone..." Owen pointed to her phone.

Sensitive, caring, a total busybody.

"You're nosy, Owen, but I still consider you like the big brother I never knew I needed." Cheyenne laughed.

"What can I say? I'm terrific like that." Owen shrugged.

There were other people at the long table, but they came and went. In truth, everyone was too tired to be chatty tonight.

Cheyenne cleaned up her end of the table and got up.

Owen followed her.

Of course, he would.

In the kitchen, she rinsed out her own plate and

silverware, plus Owen's plate and silverware, as he leaned against the counter, talking to her.

"Are you having dinner again with Roger?" he asked casually.

"And it matters to you because..." Cheyenne closed the dishwasher door, and washed her hands using the dish soap.

"I don't know. Maybe I feel responsible for putting you up to it. You should have told me *no*."

"I did. Many times over."

"Well, I guess I didn't hear it," Owen replied. "Roger hasn't said a word to me for the entire week. I waved to him at church on Sunday, but he was busy talking to Pastor Flores."

"So you want me to tell you what I think he is thinking about our non-date a week ago yesterday?" Cheyenne opened the refrigerator to get a can of soda, and then changed her mind.

It was almost eight o'clock, but there was a meeting of some importance with Captain Takayama about the fires in Savannah the last two weeks.

Everyone knew that the arsonists had struck again. Arson investigators had been working around the clock to find the suspects. Thank God that so far the fires had been contained in the city of Savannah.

Cheyenne didn't want to think about what

could possibly happen if the arsonists decided to target Tybee Island also, where the Savannah Senior Living Resort was located. She wondered how long it would take to get all the residents out of there.

She wondered whether SSLR had regular fire drills.

Surely, with Roger in charge, they would.

As much as she didn't want to, she probably had to talk to Roger soon about the safety drills.

From the corner of Cheyenne's eyes, she could see other firefighters filing into what they called their den. Someone carried a tray of cupcakes. More gifts from local residents, grateful that firefighters existed.

Cheyenne placed a palm on her stomach.

Need to lose some weight, I know. But that cupcake...

"All right. We'll talk later," Owen said.

"There's no later," Cheyenne quickly said. "Here's the summary. We had a good dinner. We talked about broken relationships. We talked about my aunt. We spent a lot of time on her problems. The end."

Owen's eyebrows went up. "That's all?"

"He was never on my radar in the first place," Cheyenne blurted. "And he probably won't ever be."

"Why not?"

Cheyenne took a deep breath. "He's... He's too good for me."

That is all.

Owen frowned. "I have a problem with what you just said."

"I don't want to know."

"I'm going to put on my Christian brother hat right now and tell you." It was as if Owen hadn't heard Cheyenne at all.

She didn't want to know.

Or did she?

"The word *good* is a trigger for me." Owen stood there, as if expecting Cheyenne to walk around him and leave the kitchen.

She didn't.

"Remember what Mark 10:18 says?" Owen asked.

"You have it memorized."

"Indeed, I have."

So Jesus said to him, "Why do you call Me good?
No one is good but One, that is, God.

"Only God is good, but you knew that," he added.

Cheyenne agreed, but she didn't nod. In her mind, she knew that Owen was right to remind her that everyone sinned.

Well, Roger seemed like he doesn't sin much.

Then again, all have sinned.

"You know the verse," Owen added.

"You read my thoughts."

"Every Christian knows that 'all have sinned and fall short of the glory of God.' Romans 3:23." Owen gestured with his hands.

Funny how he spoke with his hands a lot.

"There is no perfect man," Owen said. "Only God is perfect. But you knew that."

"The problem is perception."

"You got it. Sometimes people go the other way. Since they think there is no perfect man, then everyone must be imperfect and broken and messed up so badly that such a character is now the acceptable norm."

"What are you saying?" Cheyenne asked. "Are you both agreeing and disagreeing with me?"

"You hit the nail on the head when you said *perception.* I've heard people say, 'Oh, Christians mess up too.' Like every Christian will mess up and ruin their lives as a matter of given role. We are all sinners, yes, but it doesn't mean we will mess up all the time. As we grow in the Lord, we will want to glorify God more and more."

"So who we are now should be better than who we were, even yesterday or last week."

"Right. However, no matter how much we try to

be good Christians, we have this sin nature in us that is antagonistic toward our Holy God. Nevertheless, Christ in us has defeated this sin nature, when He nailed it to the cross."

Cheyenne nodded. "In the end, we are victorious in Christ."

"Therefore, to get back to your statement that you are 'not good enough' for Roger, in my humble opinion, your focus needs to be God, and not Roger, as wonderful and whatever he might be. Let God's perspective be your perspective."

Cheyenne drew a deep breath. "You should be a pastor."

Owen didn't reply.

"Have you considered that?" Cheyenne asked.

"I'm open to God's leading, but for now, I need to be right here. And speaking of right now, we have a meeting to attend."

Cheyenne almost forgot about it.

There was an arsonist to catch.

She followed Owen to their den, and forgot about Roger.

For now.

CHAPTER NINE

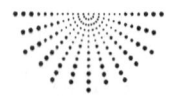

*J*ust about the only person Roger could talk to about the news was his cousin, Priyanka Jacobs.

Well, there was Diego too.

And Ming.

But right now, Roger needed a woman's perspective on what to do about the new development.

New? It wasn't truly new. The dark cloud had hung over his head for sixteen years since he had found out that he could have possibly fathered a daughter, then two years old.

Which would make that girl eighteen years old this year.

Old enough for her to leave home and do whatever she pleased.

As Roger paced his living room overlooking the vast Atlantic Ocean, he couldn't help but wonder why Victorina Mays would choose to drop out of high school one semester away from graduation.

Ironically, that supported his belief that Victorina was not his daughter, after all.

Every single Patel whom Roger knew had thought nothing about finishing college, let alone high school.

Roger glanced at the clock on the wall umpteen times. It was almost twelve o'clock. He could hear his personal chef cooking lunch in the kitchen down the hallway.

They are late!

He debated whether to text Priyanka, but it was his fault for asking the newlyweds to forego sleeping in on a Saturday morning to help him think and pray through his crisis.

Yes, indeed. This was a crisis.

As soon as he heard the doorbell, Roger half-sprinted toward the front door.

He didn't know why he was in such a hurry. After all, he had prayed fruitlessly for three days before he decided he needed to talk to someone who could maybe help him sort out his thoughts.

He hoped that Priyanka would have a fresh and objective perspective, although he wasn't sure how much Hunter could help him in this situation. Still,

Priyanka would tell her husband anyway, so might as well invite them both and feed them lunch.

I'm a practical man.

"I'm sorry we're late," Priyanka said, taking off her shoes and putting on a pair of disposable house slippers that Roger made available for his guests.

Right next to her, Hunter did the same.

Roger hadn't told them to take off their shoes. In fact, many of his non-Indian friends didn't when they stepped on his beautiful and cool Italian marble floor.

"No worries. I'm glad you could come at all," Roger said.

"Say the word and we're here." Hunter laughed.

"The word?" Roger was lost in thought.

"Food?"

"Ah, sorry. A lot on my mind."

Priyanka knitted her eyebrows together. "Let's talk."

Roger led them to his comfortable living room with the fireplace in the middle of the wall, flanked by two panels of floor-to-ceiling windows facing the ocean.

His housekeeper had opened the window panes this morning when she came to clean the house, and Roger hadn't bothered to close them.

A gentle April breeze blew in.

The waves were still dancing on the shoreline,

as they had done for thousands of years. If Roger stopped everything he was doing, he could hear the ocean.

Something he hadn't been paying attention to for many years.

Confining himself to his office at SSLR would do that, he supposed. It also prevented him from actually enjoying his beach home that Ming's wife, a real estate agent extraordinaire, had helped him to purchase some years ago.

What's the point of a nice big oceanfront house that I can't enjoy?

Well, he could enjoy it, but...

There were always problems to solve, fires to put out...

Speaking of fires, Roger wondered how his favorite firefighter was doing. It had been three days since they had last texted each other.

The next day, Cheyenne stopped by SSLR to see her aunt, but Roger was in a meeting.

Hunter stood at one of the tall windows. "Wow. We've come here many times, but I still can't get over this view and the sounds of the ocean."

His wife wove her arm through his. "It's amazing."

"At the yurt, you can't even hear the road on the other side of the trees, let alone the ocean way—over there somewhere." Hunter kissed the side of Priyanka's head.

Watching the married couple, Roger felt a longing in his heart.

Will there be someone like that for me someday?

Even as he asked God, he was sure it wasn't meant to be. He was sure he was going to be a bachelor the rest of his life.

Considering what he had done, those skeletons in his closets back in the days when he had been a new baby Christian—

That's exactly it.

Roger would have a proper excuse if he had not been saved when he and Mimi had sinned together in that small apartment of hers across from their medical school.

However, he had been saved since high school.

He had no excuse.

I'm a prodigal son through and through.

CHAPTER TEN

*R*oger didn't want his personal chef and the kitchen staff to hear about his dirty little secret, although the child that had resulted was innocently pure.

He waited until after lunch, after the crew had cleaned up the dining room and kitchen, and left, before he led Priyanka and Hunter back to his living room.

Ironically, Roger had no trouble eating lunch.

He had learned to compartmentalize his life over the years, to separate what he wanted to deal with from that which he wanted to lock in the attic and throw away the key.

After the kitchen staff had left, Roger made hot tea for his guests.

They sat in the living room as he told them a somewhat sanitized summary of his dalliances in medical school, praying the entire time that his other former girlfriends hadn't gotten pregnant without his knowledge.

Oddly enough, Priyanka and Hunter had listened without any apparent negative reaction.

Roger thought that it might be due to the years Priyanka had worked in the ER. She had seen and heard everything.

As for Hunter, who knew? Maybe his being a novelist meant he had researched on just about anything, including the lurid and unbelievable—or unbelievably stupid.

There was a reason God had meant for intimacies to be confined to a marriage bed.

Not before.

And certainly not outside of marriage.

Roger handed Priyanka his phone with the photograph of Victorina on it. It was dated two years ago, and the girl had fluorescent blue hair. Her facial features reminded him of...

"That server at Piper's Place," Priyanka exclaimed.

Roger sighed. "She's already here. She hasn't approached me or anything. Hasn't called SSLR or inquired about me."

"She's biding her time or something?" Priyanka

passed the phone to Hunter, who had actually been looking over her shoulder at the same image.

"Pastor Hiram taught me that it's best to know what God thinks about a situation before we make decisions about it," Priyanka said.

"That's wise." Roger nodded.

It wasn't something he hadn't heard before. In fact, he himself had taught his Sunday School class about seeking God's will in every area of their lives, rather than go off doing something without God's blessings.

Ah, Sunday School.

How could I teach it now that my secret is out?

He caught himself asking the wrong question.

How could I teach it at all, whether I have secrets or not?

For we have all sinned and fallen short of the glory of God...

"May I ask you something?" Hunter leaned back in the oversized sofa.

Roger nodded. At this point, he could take on anything. He had felt the gamut of shame for the last three days. *Bring it on.*

"You kept saying it's a crisis, but how could it be a crisis if you've known about this for sixteen years?" Hunter asked.

"Well, the cat is out of the bag now," Priyanka said before Roger did.

Roger took a deep breath.

"Like I said, when Ming told me that Mimi had blackmailed five men into paying support for one child, I wanted to believe so badly that she's not mine." Shame filled Roger's entire body. "Now that she has arrived, is working at Piper's Place, in front of all our church friends, the confrontation is inevitable."

Suddenly Hunter smiled. "You're a father, Roger."

"I don't know yet. I want the DNA test redone."

"How long has she been in town?" Hunter asked.

"I don't know, and frankly, I don't care. I just..."

I just want her to go away.

But she's a child—

No, she's not. She's eighteen.

A fully grown adult who can live her own life apart from her parents, biological or not.

"I don't know why she's even here." Roger stretched out on the couch. "There are five men, people. Five! Mimi has no idea who her daughter's dad really is. So here's this girl, trekking across the country, looking for her biological father."

"If you were in her shoes, wouldn't you want to know who your real dad is?" Priyanka asked.

"I'm not in her shoes," Roger snapped.

Hunter raised his hand. "Will she agree to submit to a new DNA test?"

"She has to. I will pay for it. In fact, I'll pay for all five men to take the test if it turns out that she's not mine. I don't care how much it costs. I have to know. Someone has to take responsibility for this mess. If she's not my daughter, then I can go my merry way. She won't be my responsibility."

"She's eighteen, you said," Priyanka reminded him. "You're only responsible for child support, not adult support."

Still...

A daughter.

Nah. She's not mine.

Roger was surprised at his own resolution. Was he trying to compartmentalize this again, as he had done for so many years?

"Let's pray for God to give you wisdom about this," Hunter said.

"Thank you." Roger was grateful that God had brought Hunter into Priyanka's life. Roger was glad to see the two of them happily married.

Ah, marriage is not for me.

Roger had too much sin baggage to be the best husband for anyone. Surely his punishment was to be single the rest of his life.

Punishment?

Bachelorhood wasn't a punishment if God had called him to such a life.

He had been celibate since Mimi, and that had been such a long time ago, that he had forgotten how to love a woman.

Love?

He hadn't loved Mimi. No, not really.

He didn't remember what they had, if anything at all. She had been convenient. They had studied together in medical school, spent too much time with each other, done too many things together.

Roger prayed that Victorina would not sin like her parents—

Parents?

Of which I am not one.

Slowly, Roger realized that Hunter was praying. His own head bowed, but he hadn't heard the first half of what Hunter had prayed. God heard it though, and that was enough for him.

For such a time as this, when he could hardly pray, God had sent other Christians to pray for him.

How merciful is our God!

How merciful!

Roger held back tears.

His focus crystalized, and Roger listened quietly as Hunter kept praying. After he prayed, his wife prayed such a beautiful prayer for the girl to come to know Jesus as her personal Lord and Savior, if she hadn't already.

They waited for Roger to pray, but he couldn't. All he could say was, "Amen."

"Have you talked to Pastor Flores?" Priyanka asked. "Of course, we all know that it is God on whom we need to rely—not on pastors or counselors or ourselves. But Pastor Flores might have insight, and you could give him an update."

"I will." Roger sipped his still-hot tea. "Want more tea?"

Nonchalantly, like.

Roger couldn't believe how he had eased back to his old ways of dealing with bad news. Push it aside, wait for the fallout, react like it was no big deal.

The tougher the situation, the more he blocked it out and tried not to think about it.

On the other hand, how would God want him to deal with problems?

What had he himself taught his Sunday School class the last ten years?

Had it all been a lie?

Repent! Repent! Repent!

The flood of tears came.

There was nothing Roger could do about it. He pulled his tee shirt collar over his chin to cover his face, and he wept into the soft cotton that cost him five hundred dollars retail.

All the while, an eighteen-year-old had lived her entire life without a father and without a properly planned future.

A high school dropout.

No Patel would ever do that, he repeated to himself.

Therefore, that girl could never be a Patel.

Not my daughter.

CHAPTER ELEVEN

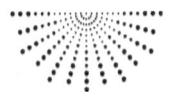

*S*aturday night at Piper's Place.

What was I thinking?

Cheyenne sat in the corner booth that over-looked River Street, feeling guilty that she had taken up the entire table all by herself, while a bunch of people were probably downstairs, waiting to be seated on this busy night.

Still, Piper's policy had never been money-oriented.

As the story went, Piper Peyton had been led to Christ by Heidi Wei-Flores, the pastor's wife, the first day she had attended church so many years ago.

She had been at Riverside Chapel ever since, being active in many ministries.

Her latest ministry was to feed the poor and house the homeless. Pastor Flores had let her organize and run their new Riverside Village ministry to do just that.

From time to time during her time off, Cheyenne would help Piper raise funds or help in whatever way she could in the ministry. Piper had told her that she could come to Piper's Place at any time and be seated.

Priority seating.

Just like the airplane—

Cheyenne closed her eyes over her cup of decaffeinated coffee.

Why does every thought of airplane and airports remind me of Roger paying for her plane ticket?

It had been more than three years ago.

No point belaboring an old good deed.

After all, Roger had told her to forget it.

She ate her Belgian waffles slowly.

Yes, waffles.

Cheyenne didn't know why she had ordered waffles at nine o'clock in the evening.

Well, since she worked twenty-four-hour shifts —with overtime, thanks to the arsonists—her night and day sometimes blurred together. She had had steak at breakfast and pancakes at night.

Waffles with gobs of strawberries and whipped cream on top, with slight puffs of sugar... Yum!

The server came to refill her coffee. "How's everything?"

Leila.

The same server whom Cheyenne had seen for the first time almost two weeks ago, when she had a non-date dinner with Roger.

Thing was, she wasn't the server who had taken Cheyenne's order, though. What happened to that guy?

"I'm filling in for Monte," Leila explained, as if she knew Cheyenne was curious. "May I get you more coffee? More syrup? Another waffle?"

"Maybe just more coffee."

As Leila refilled her cup, Cheyenne decided to broach the subject. "Where are you from, Leila?"

"Oh, everywhere. My mother moved from state to state, and we all went with her. Minors couldn't be choosers and all that, you know?"

Cheyenne noted the past tense.

Moved.

Went.

"She still moves around, but I'm done," Leila added.

"Oh?"

"Yeah. Every time she got a divorce, we moved to another state. She wanted a new beginning, as if all that could wash away what was."

Whoa.

That was a lot of information that Cheyenne hadn't expected.

Perhaps Leila was so lonely that she'd open up to a still-stranger such as Cheyenne. Perhaps this was the only table with one single customer who had nobody else to talk to.

Both of them, alone.

Perhaps God had brought them here for such a time as this.

"That must be hard on you," Cheyenne said quietly.

"I don't know. If it's a life you're used to, you might not know of better ways."

"That's profound."

"Is it?" Leila shrugged. "However, that part of my life is over now. When I turned eighteen, I high-tailed out of there. I got tired of babysitting my four half-siblings pro bono."

Bitterness there?

"How did you end up in Savannah?" Cheyenne asked, being careful not to suggest or direct the conversation.

"I'm looking for my dad."

"Your dad?" Cheyenne tried not to speculate.

"Well, biological father. He may not know I exist."

"Oh."

"I want to just see him. Talk to him. That's all." Her voice sounded unsure.

"And?"

"I saw someone, but he didn't recognize me." Leila shrugged. "I don't know if he's actually my dad. But each of us has one real biological dad, and I'm determined to find him."

"Did you say hello or something?" Cheyenne remembered that evening when she and Roger had eaten dinner together here.

Leila's features still reminded Cheyenne of Roger Patel.

What was the probability of that?

It couldn't be random.

It had to be planned.

"How long have you been looking for your dad?" Cheyenne asked.

"Only two weeks, but I've been planning this for a while. I had to wait until I turned eighteen. I didn't want to get into trouble."

Planned.

What did I say?

Somehow this girl knew to come here. "How did you figure that your dad might be in Savannah?"

"Mom gave me a few—several—names." She took a deep breath, like she was holding back tears.

Cheyenne couldn't imagine having several possible dads.

"So I'm like, guessing my way through," Leila said. "I don't know what I'm doing. I hope to earn enough money waiting tables to pay for DNA tests."

"Well, that sounds like a good start." Cheyenne sipped her coffee. By now her waffle was cold, but she didn't care. "I'm sorry for what you've been through."

"Life is always hard, isn't it?"

"At least you know your mother, and you grew up with her for eighteen years."

"I guess. She did her best."

"I was adopted," Cheyenne said. Usually, she was a private person, but this girl needed to know that she wasn't the only person in the world with family problems.

"You were?" Leila's eyes brightened. "Did you know your real dad?"

"Actually, no. My biological mother left me at the post office."

Leila's palm covered her mouth, and her big brown eyes seemed to grow a size larger. "What?"

"You could say I was delivered."

"First class?" Leila gasped. "Sorry. Sorry. I didn't mean to..."

Cheyenne shrugged. "You should see the jokes at the fire station."

"You work in a fire station?"

"I'm a firefighter."

"Wow. A first responder. Much respect." Leila did a slight salute. "I'm sorry again. I was just thinking I have such a hard life, and now I find out yours is worse."

"I'm glad I could cheer you up."

A server with silver hair and silver nose ring passed by, quickly whispering in Leila's ears.

She frowned. "Ah, the manager is watching me."

"Oh no. I'm sorry."

"I better go," Leila said. "They don't pay me to chat."

"Maybe we can have coffee sometime, after you finish work," Cheyenne offered.

"I'd like that. Then you can tell me how you got from the post office to the fire station."

"Sure." Cheyenne was happy she could cheer her up, even a little.

"If you need another waffle or more syrup, please let me know," Leila said quickly.

"I'm fine. Thank you."

Leila slipped away so quickly that Cheyenne couldn't stop her.

I'm looking for my dad.

How odd. Or was it?

Sometimes people looked for their children, parents, relatives, family members. Every year, many people were lost and not found.

Fighting fires all over Savannah and Tybee Island, Cheyenne had a glimpse of the slice of life of the common man.

We have all been tainted by Adam's sin. We have all suffered the curse of that sin upon this earth.

Some more than others.

Cheyenne recalled how she had lost her own adopted parents too, when she had been very young. God had spared her, truly. Since she had been too little to comprehend the loss of two parents, she had led a very happy childhood, living with her Aunt Gemma and Uncle Rupert.

A very happy childhood indeed.

That was, until middle school, when Aunt Gemma sat down and explained her entire life story, from the time she had been abandoned by a teenage mother, to her eventual adoption by a couple who couldn't have children of their own.

And yet, thank God that she had loving homes to grow up in.

She wondered what sort of childhood Leila had, moving from place to place. Such instability to impose on a child.

Still, God had been gracious to her as well.

Thank You, Jesus.

Cheyenne prayed that God would show her how she could minister to Leila. That girl might not know the love of Jesus Christ. She might not have the peace of God in her heart.

Even if she were a Christian, she might still need encouragement.

A friend in a lonely land.

CHAPTER TWELVE

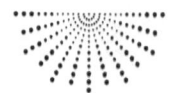

*W*hen Roger spotted Cheyenne and her aunt strolling in the greenhouse, he stayed out of sight and walked down another path back to his office.

He wanted to talk to Cheyenne about his project, but he couldn't risk more teases from Miss Gemma.

He had to find a way to talk to Cheyenne after she had dropped off her aunt back in her room.

He texted her.

And then he went back to his office to wait.

He couldn't focus on the work at hand, that pile of SSLR projects he had to deal with. Papers to sign, scholarship applications to read, problems to resolve, schedules to set.

He wished his administrative assistant hadn't

been on maternity leave, and that his temporary assistant hadn't quit.

How hard can it be to find help these days?

Roger thanked God that Priyanka was an efficient assistant director who had helped him sort out some of the issues he had been unable to overcome the last few years.

That was the big difference between him and his cousin.

While Roger looked at everything with a broad art brush from a CEO-like point of view, Priyanka was more into details, like a chief operating officer.

God had been merciful to him, as Priyanka covered all the details he had missed.

Plus, she had great bedside manners, and SSLR residents loved her—perhaps more than they liked him.

The knock on his door startled him.

He had left the door open while he waited for Cheyenne.

And here she was.

"You rang?" Cheyenne smiled.

That smile.

Roger stared a little bit. He had to. Cheyenne had a smile that seemed to say, *Everything is going to be okay. It's just a small fire. We can put it out.*

"You got my message." Roger offered her a seat. "Anything to drink?"

"No, I'm fine." Cheyenne adjusted her cross-body purse. "What is it about? It sounded urgent."

Roger poured coffee from a carafe that someone had left for him. It was two in the afternoon, and he'd downed at least one whole carafe of coffee. Maybe one more cup, and he'd better stop.

Before he returned to his desk, he stopped at the door. "I need to close this door because this is a private conversation, but I don't want to close the door if you feel uncomfortable being in the room alone with me."

"Is this a matter that concerns us or other people?"

"Other people."

"Ah, we don't want gossips to start."

Roger nodded.

"Can you say enough with the door ajar slightly such that we can go forward?" Cheyenne asked.

"I don't know."

"If you have to go cryptic and I have no clue what you're saying, then I say we need to adjourn the meeting to another time when we could talk, or when we have someone else with us you can trust."

"Okay."

"What on earth is this about? Now I'm super curious." Cheyenne kept her voice down.

Roger still stood at the door, one hand holding

his coffee mug, the other hand on the door knob. "Maybe this is a mistake."

"Something seems to be bothering you, so if you feel that I am the one you need to talk to, here I am." Cheyenne splayed her hands on her knees.

"You're a good friend," Roger said.

"Only God is good," Cheyenne replied. "He is the best solution to our problem."

Our problem.

Roger felt as though Cheyenne had placed her palm on his chest.

He didn't know anyone else who was helpful all the time. When someone was in need, and God placed her there, she went all out to help them.

No wonder she was a firefighter.

Perhaps that was her calling.

More than that, she was called to help people.

And now I need all the help I can get.

"Is Priyanka at work?" Cheyenne asked.

"Yes. Why?"

"Is this something she can be privy to?"

"She already knows about it."

"Good. Then she can sit in with us and we can close the door."

Roger felt embarrassed. "I should have thought of that."

"That's why I'm here, I think. I'm your Samwise."

"Am I Frodo, then?" Roger chuckled. "The one who has to carry the ring of doom?"

~

*I*t had turned out that Priyanka was too busy to sit in on a meeting between Roger and Cheyenne in the SSLR Director's office.

Besides, Priyanka reminded Roger that he was on company time, and that this was a private matter. She said it right in front of Cheyenne.

And yet, Cheyenne didn't make a face at Roger, and didn't say anything unkind to him.

Roger felt that Cheyenne was the most non-judgmental person he knew.

Still, he had a feeling that once Cheyenne found out about his past, she would change her mind about him.

Sure, she had said she wanted to help, but to what extent?

No point speculating now.

After work the same day, Roger had gone home to his house down the road from SSLR, changed into tee shirt and jeans, and then drove to the Chinese restaurant, where he was getting a takeout for four people.

Priyanka and Hunter had invited Roger to have

his meeting at their yurt at Jacobs Landing, south of where Roger lived.

It was the right thing to do.

This was a private matter, like Priyanka had reminded him back at his office. It had nothing to do with SSLR.

I'm suddenly unable to function.

The entire Victorina situation had clouded his days at work. Every waking moment, he wondered what to do about her arrival in town.

Perhaps if she were still visiting the other father candidates, Roger could put off thinking about the ramifications.

He certainly hadn't thought of all these things when he and Mimi had messed up so many years ago.

Sowing and reaping.

CHAPTER THIRTEEN

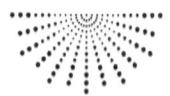

*a*pril evenings on Tybee Island were Cheyenne's favorite time of the year. The temperature hovered between afternoon warm and midnight cool, and the stars were gorgeous after the clouds rolled by.

Stretched out on the wicker lounge on Priyanka's deck overlooking the pond behind her yurt, Cheyenne faced the night sky, digesting her dinner and dessert.

She had probably eaten one too many cupcakes, but in all fairness, she needed the food fuel to help her handle whatever it was that had bothered Roger all day long—and perhaps longer.

He was nowhere to be found at this time.

The lounge chair on the other side of the side table was empty. That was where he was supposed to sit after dinner, and ask her for help about the project he had in mind.

Cheyenne heard people talking inside the yurt behind her. Roger, Hunter, and Priyanka were in the kitchen.

She didn't hear anyone laugh. Or cry.

Waiting for Roger, Cheyenne began to pray.

"Lord Jesus, I don't know what is bothering Roger. It must be something serious, although I've always thought that it's nice for some people not to have a lot of strife in life, like I've been through."

Praying about strife reminded Cheyenne of Leila.

"I pray for Leila. Some broken family she's had, and she's only eighteen. She seems to be looking for a place to belong. I pray that she will find perfect peace in Jesus Christ."

Before she could continue, the door opened.

"Sorry to keep you waiting." Roger walked around Cheyenne to the other lounge.

Then he didn't say anything for a good minute.

They simply stared up into the night sky.

Surely he hadn't called Cheyenne here only for a family dinner and star gazing.

Cheyenne had never been to Priyanka's home, and she wasn't sure if she'd ever come back. While she knew Priyanka from her interactions with Aunt Gemma, they were no more than church friends, running into each other every now and then.

She hardly knew Hunter, though she had seen him around at SSLR, working landscape and doing maintenance. Aunt Gemma said that he also worked part time at the front office at Jacobs Landing, assisting his aunt as she ran this vacation spot.

As for Roger, Cheyenne had known him for a few years now.

Sometimes God brought people together in unexpected situations, and they remained friends for a while.

How long is a while?

She couldn't begin to guess.

Roger cleared his throat.

Like he was going to make a speech or something.

"I need a favor," Roger said.

Cheyenne turned her head toward him. "Finally."

"I never wanted to ask for something in return for anything, but I need your help."

"If it's within my ability to do it, and if it doesn't go against God, then let's hear it." Cheyenne meant it. The last thing she'd want to do was anything that God did not approve.

"Remember the girl at Piper's Place who waited

at our table a couple of weeks ago?" Roger said slowly.

"Has it been a couple of weeks ago?"

"Yeah. Feels like recently. Do you happen to know if she still works there? I mean, have you been back there since our dinner?"

"Yes and yes."

Roger scratched his head. "What's her name again?"

"Leila."

Roger produced a phone. Handed it to Cheyenne. "See the resemblance?"

Cheyenne wasn't sure where this was going. "Look at that neon blue hair."

"Is that what it was? That photo was taken two years ago." Roger waved his hand. "Cover up her hair and tell me if that looks like Leila."

It sure did. Cheyenne handed the phone back to Roger. "What is this about?"

Roger cleared his throat again.

Somewhere in the distance, beyond the citronella candles, the deck, grass, and pond, frogs called out in the dark.

Behind them, the yurt was silent.

"To be sure, this has absolutely nothing to do with you," Roger said. "But I felt that since we have both seen her together, we could show up together, and it will make it easier for me to carry it out."

"Carry out what?"

CHAPTER FOURTEEN

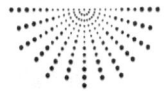

*I*nterrupted at every sentence by those distant frogs on the other side of the pond, Roger said as much as he felt he could, without embarrassing himself any further in front of a lady he might have wanted to date.

Maybe if the circumstances had been different.

Silence fell between them.

Except for the frogs.

He wondered what sort of frogs they were, but this wasn't the time to chase rabbit trails.

"Say something," Roger said.

Under the dim wall light behind them, casting a pale glow on Cheyenne's face, she looked like she was about to cry.

But she suddenly steeled her face.

Maybe *steeled* wasn't the right word, but neither was *rigid*.

In any case, Roger couldn't read Cheyenne's mind.

"I'm sorry, Cheyenne," Roger said. "I let you down."

Cheyenne didn't say a word.

Maybe she was thinking about how to respond, how to help?

"I know that many people attend my Sunday School class, thinking I have so much wisdom to dispense, when all I am is a broken vessel with skeletons popping out of my closet. It is by the mercy and grace of God that I am here at all."

Still, not a word from Cheyenne.

"Are you asleep?" Roger asked.

"No."

"Okay. I just want to add that I talked to Diego about it too, and we both agree that we need to wait and see what the DNA results are. That is, if we can get Leila a.k.a. Victorina to do a DNA test."

"And you talked to Priyanka and Hunter," Cheyenne said.

"Yes. I also talked to my old friend, Ming, who knew about some part of this."

"And?"

"And what?" Roger asked.

"And who else did you talk to?" Cheyenne asked.

"That's all."

"No, that shouldn't be all."

"Huh?" Roger sat up.

"Did you talk to God?" Cheyenne asked him.

"Of course, I talked to God. I prayed and asked Him to forgive me and help me out of this mess."

Cheyenne also sat up. "May I be frank with you, Roger?"

"Yes, please."

"You just listed to me all the people you talked to, but God wasn't the first Person you mentioned. In fact, I had to coax that out of you. If God is on the forefront, then you would have said you prayed to God first."

"Well, I did."

"But how much percentage of time did you spend with God over this matter?"

Roger sighed. "You're right. I spent more time worrying and chatting about it than praying, to tell you the honest truth. I was concerned about my reputation as a Sunday School teacher. I think I let our church down."

It was a good thing that Cheyenne wasn't in his class. Roger hoped that she could be objective about this problem of his.

"I was also concerned about what SSLR residents would think." Roger closed his eyes. "I already know what God thinks of me. But you're right. I'm embarrassed in front of my peers and other Christians. And you."

"Me?" Cheyenne folded her arms across her chest.

Roger pointed at her action. "See there? You might be thinking poorly of me right now."

"Read my mind, why don't you? What am I thinking now, exactly?" Cheyenne asked.

Roger didn't want to make her upset, but he wanted Cheyenne to think well of him.

"You wondered how I could be such a sinner."

"We are all sinners. 'For all have sinned and fall short of the glory of God.' Romans 3:23, remember?" Cheyenne responded.

"Yeah."

"And you know what Romans 6:23 says."

For the wages of sin is death, but the gift of God is eternal life in Christ Jesus our Lord.

"I know. I get your point, Cheyenne. "Sin is sin."

"But God forgives. *That* is my point."

Cheyenne's voice was quiet, but it cut Roger like a razor blade.

Galatians 6:7-8 flooded into his memory.

Do not be deceived, God is not mocked; for whatever a man sows, that he will also reap. For he who sows to his flesh will of the flesh reap corruption, but he who sows to the Spirit will of the Spirit reap everlasting life.

"I've disappointed you," Roger said, repeating himself.

"Well... Don't get me wrong. I need time to process this. It's easier since we're not dating or anything."

"I guess." And now they might never date.

"Right now, we don't know for sure if Leila is Victorina. If she is, then your sin is nineteen years old. If you have asked God to forgive you of it, then He has. The only big problem now is the consequences of your actions, which you can't avoid."

"I know."

"What's our plan?" Cheyenne asked, seemingly moving on. "You want us to go back to Piper's Place often to befriend Leila and get a DNA test out of her, I'm gathering?"

Our plan?

Roger swallowed bile in his throat. He had dragged Cheyenne—beautiful Cheyenne—into his ugliness.

"First, we need to know if she's Victorina,"

Cheyenne continued. "And we can't ask Piper for personnel records because they're not for outsiders."

"Ming is on it. He has other means to find out via his PI connections." Roger wondered how much to tell Cheyenne. Why not? "I'm also asking Ming to send someone to keep an eye on her. See what she does off hours."

"The last thing you need is an extortion or blackmail."

The way she said it, Roger couldn't tell if she was joking or serious.

She moved on to the next question. "If she turns out to be your daughter?"

"Then we'll go from there. If it's money she needs or something, I can make arrangements to deal with it."

"I've talked to her about her family," Cheyenne said, relating to Roger what Leila had told her. "Seems that she just wants to belong. To know where she came from."

"Is that all? There must be more than that."

Cheyenne looked at him. "Not everyone wants money, you know."

"Of course not. I'm just saying that I don't know her."

"So we go to Piper's Place, sit there, let her come to talk to us, and see what she's going to do."

"Yeah, it's better than for her to suddenly show up at SSLR or my house," Roger said.

"You don't know if she will still do that."

"That's why I'm increasing security at my house."

"She looks harmless," Cheyenne said. "I think she needs Jesus."

Roger was stunned.

Then he felt ashamed.

He bowed his head.

"Are you okay?" Cheyenne asked.

Roger nodded.

But he was far from okay.

I think she needs Jesus.

That should have been his thought first. Yet, he hadn't even thought about Leila's spiritual condition. All he had thought about for days was damage control.

Lord Jesus, forgive me for I have sinned.

CHAPTER FIFTEEN

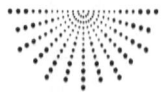

*A*fter all the trouble Cheyenne went through of coordinating Roger's schedule with hers so that they could have another make-believe dinner at Piper's Place, they arrived at the same time, driving different vehicles, only to find out that Leila had been fired.

"Oh no. I'm sorry." Cheyenne's heart dropped to the wood floor.

"For chatting up customers on the clock," the silver-haired twenty-something explained. She still wore the same type of nose ring that she had worn that day when Cheyenne spotted her whispering warnings to Leila when the latter had stopped too long at Cheyenne's table.

"When?"

"Last night."

"So soon. She might still be in town, then?" Cheyenne felt bad.

"Don't know." Silver Hair stepped away. "She can't pay her rent, so who knows where she is now."

Cheyenne glanced at Roger standing quietly next to her, wondering how he had reacted to that piece of information.

She can't pay her rent.

His supposed daughter couldn't pay the rent. Was she out in the streets?

Roger wasn't looking at her. He was texting on his phone.

Cheyenne waited.

When he looked up, he sighed. "Ming's going to call me when he finds something. He knows how to find missing people."

Cheyenne left Roger standing there as she went after Silver Hair, who had just finished taking orders from some customers.

Cheyenne pressed a twenty into the server's palm. "Do you have Leila's phone number?"

Silver Hair didn't say anything.

Cheyenne gave her another twenty. "That's all I have."

It was enough.

"She never said not to give out her number." Silver Hair justified it before she vanished into the kitchen.

Cheyenne texted Leila, reminded her who she was, and asked to meet for lunch.

Leila didn't reply right away.

Cheyenne returned to Roger, still standing under the exit sign, looking stoic.

"She talked?" Roger asked quietly, as if they were doing something hush-hush.

"I got her number, and we'll see where we go from there."

"I've lost my appetite."

"I haven't. We're already here. Why don't we get a table?" Cheyenne suggested. "You can watch me eat."

Roger stared at her. Cheyenne thought his eyebrows relaxed a bit.

"Well..."

Cheyenne stopped him from saying more. "We drove separately. You can leave if you want, but I haven't eaten dinner."

"Neither have I."

"And here we are, surrounded by food."

"Good point."

"So let's eat?"

Roger hesitated. Then he nodded. "I'm sorry I'm in a bad state."

"You're a dude in distress." She laughed.

"And you're my lady in shining armor?" Roger frowned.

"Since we're not doing business here—with Leila not around—we'll go dutch, okay?" Cheyenne offered.

"No, no. We agreed. I'm paying for dinner, and I'm keeping my word."

"But you're not eating."

"Dinner is still on me. As agreed." Roger reached for her hand and led the way toward the hostess station.

~

"Are you sure you want to do this?" Cheyenne asked as they exited Piper's Place after a hearty dinner.

Roger could barely walk down the sidewalk. Yes, he had said he wasn't hungry. Yes, he had eaten anyway. That chicken pot pie was to *diet* for.

"What are you saying? That I'm waddling?" Roger glared at Cheyenne.

She chuckled. "No, no. I'm going to repeat myself: you don't have to come with me. I can very well go to the shops myself. There aren't too many to check."

"In the dark?" Roger pointed to the sky.

"It's only nine o'clock. Besides, the street lamps light the way. I'll be fine."

"A woman walking alone?"

"Come on." Cheyenne reached for something in her purse, and retrieved a small hairband. She tied her loose hair up into a chignon.

"Whew. I thought you were checking to see if your concealed weapon is there," Roger whispered in her ear.

"What? No."

"You don't carry?"

"Not these days."

"Maybe you should."

Cheyenne gave him an odd look. "What's going on, Roger? Too much high carb from the chicken pot pie?"

Roger shook his head. "I don't know. I don't know."

"Look over there at that street corner."

Roger did as he was told.

"See the police officer there?"

Roger nodded.

"Keep looking and you will see more police officers. It's totally safe. Savannah wants to protect its visitors. Tourism is a huge industry here, as you know."

Roger drew a deep breath. "I don't know what overcame me."

He didn't remember the last time he felt this protective of anyone. Well, maybe of his cousin Priyanka when she had been dating that loser of a boyfriend several years ago. She was married now to a man who loved God. Roger was happy for her. For them both.

Next to his cousin, Cheyenne was the closest person he felt he needed to watch out for. It wasn't because of her aunt, Miss Gemma, at all.

Roger was sure that it was because of Cheyenne herself, her nature to give and help. Even now, on her night off, she had agreed to help Roger deal with the possibly long lost daughter of his.

A whole evening gone for his sake.

And he wasn't even family.

At this hour, almost getting too late to be out at night on River Street, Cheyenne was still helping. She wanted to get a surprise gift for Miss Gemma, who couldn't come to River Street herself.

"Maybe Aunt Gemma would like a pink tee shirt that says Savannah. What do you think?" Cheyenne asked.

Roger wasn't sure why she asked for his opinion. She knew her own aunt better than anyone else. Perhaps she wanted to make small talk or something.

"Well, she has a lot of pink stuff, including a pink wheelchair. Maybe a different color might not be so jarring to the eye," Roger said.

Cheyenne was quiet.

"You regret asking me," Roger added. "In fact, I

retract what I said because I don't have a clue what women want, especially your aunt."

They stopped at the edge of the sidewalk, waiting for a car to pass.

On the other side of the road, there were several souvenir shops that opened until ten o'clock or midnight, or so Cheyenne had told him when they had been eating dinner at Piper's Place.

"I'm beginning to think you have a point," Cheyenne said. "Aunt Gemma could use a splash of color. She likes daffodils, so maybe a yellow shirt."

Roger shrugged. "To be honest, I have no idea, and I don't want to be blamed if she hates it."

"You won't be blamed," Cheyenne assured him.

You won't be blamed.

Roger wondered if this was one of the few times in his life when he would be blameless. He had done so many things in his life that he was ashamed of.

But here was Cheyenne, still his friend.

Or at least she had given him the impression that she was still his friend.

His heart heavy, Roger slowed down.

Cheyenne motioned for him to keep up. "Come on. Let's go before some of the shops close."

The rest of the walk was a blur as Roger followed Cheyenne in and out of the souvenir shops, looking for that yellow tee shirt that might please Miss Gemma.

When they passed an ice cream shop, Roger stopped. "Want ice cream?"

"Not staying healthy?" Cheyenne asked.

"Who said we are? I just had a whole chicken pot pie."

Cheyenne laughed. "Might as well go all the way?"

Roger sobered. "Maybe we shouldn't. I'm not thinking straight."

"Maybe you've had a long day. Maybe ice cream could help."

Roger changed his mind. "No, it can't."

Cheyenne seemed to be waiting for him to say more.

"Truth be told, I need to spend more time in the Word of God," Roger confessed. "My mind is going everywhere but His Word these days. I'm looking for distractions."

"Is eating a distraction?"

"I don't know."

Cheyenne blinked. "Am I a distraction?"

The question caught Roger by surprise. He opened his mouth and no word came out.

Cheyenne started to walk away.

Roger went after her.

She didn't turn to see if he was keeping up. She simply kept walking.

Did I hurt her feelings?

Roger couldn't tell. He caught up with her. Reached for her arm. "Cheyenne."

She didn't answer. Neither did she pull away.

Roger stepped in front of her. Right under another old street lamp.

Her hair was somewhat glowing under the light. He could see her eyelashes. Her eyes were dark. Her cheeks looked soft in the night light. So soft he wanted to touch them.

But he didn't.

"Cheyenne," he whispered. "You're never a distraction. I think you're a gift of God for this time in my life right now. I thank God for you."

Cheyenne nodded. "I'm sorry I was a bit sensitive. It's night time and I want to get the tee shirt and go home."

"Maybe I can drive you home."

"No. My car will be stuck at the parking lot overnight, and who knows how much that's going to cost me tomorrow. Besides, I need to get back to my shift tomorrow."

The gravity of Cheyenne's sacrifice was not lost on Roger. "You took your day off to help me. You didn't need to. I really appreciate it."

"I'm doing it for the Lord, even though it's a favor I owed you."

Roger nodded. "I am also reaping the overflowing benefits of your generosity."

Cheyenne looked at him earnestly. "Help me find a yellow shirt for Aunt Gemma in forty minutes, and we can call it a night."

"Okay. Let's do it." And the short mission was a small little distraction that Roger needed. It might be insignificant to others, but to Roger, it helped.

Thank God for blessings big and small.

Thank God for them all.

CHAPTER SIXTEEN

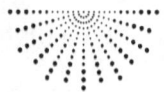

Cheyenne figured that the best place for them to have lunch was at the small public park next door to the fire station. It had a couple of picnic tables under shady trees, and was generally empty midweek.

"I'm sorry I got you fired from Piper's Place," Cheyenne said over her quinoa salad in a box.

Across from Cheyenne, Leila seemed to make an effort chewing the quinoa salad. She kept drinking water, as if she was swallowing the bits of cucumber and tomato whole.

"I should have made you a sandwich," Cheyenne said.

"Apology not accepted." Leila smiled. "You shared your lunch. I'm grateful. I haven't eaten since last night—I mean, thank you very much."

On that note, Cheyenne would've offered Leila the rest of her lunch.

Once she had tracked down Leila and invited her to lunch, it had to be at Leila's convenience, or Cheyenne might lose the transient eighteen-year-old.

When Leila said she'd meet Cheyenne for lunch, it happened on the day the latter was at work.

"You didn't get me fired. It's not your fault." Leila drank more water. "The manager hates me, is all."

Cheyenne didn't know what went on at Piper's Place, or at restaurants in general, so she had no opinion about it.

"I'm glad you texted me back," Cheyenne said. "I wasn't sure if you would, considering I got your number from your friend, and not directly."

"It's okay, but forty dollars is too much to pay her for my number. We could've exchanged numbers when I was still at Piper's, you know."

"I had no idea they were going to let you go so soon."

"Me neither."

"Thanks for having lunch with me."

"Sorry it took two days to meet with you. I had to try to find a job. Unfortunately there was none for me."

Cheyenne watched the girl suffer through her super healthy salad.

"Where did you stay last night?" Cheyenne asked, remembering that Silver Hair had said Leila couldn't pay her rent.

"I found a place."

"Where?"

"You don't have to know."

"I want to know. I feel responsible. Maybe I could talk to Piper Peyton for you. She could give you your job back—"

"No. Please don't." Chewing slowly, Leila somehow finished her entire plate of salad. "That wasn't too bad. You know, I don't like tomatoes."

"Oh." Cheyenne felt even worse now.

"But beggars can't be choosers."

"You're not a beggar."

"I've always been a beggar since before I was ever born." Leila's voice shook. "I fought to survive when my own mother tried to abort me."

"Wow." Cheyenne's jaw dropped.

"They thought I wouldn't make it. Once I was born, my mother had to keep me, you know. State laws and all that. Years later, when I found out what had happened, I knew without a doubt that my own mother hated me. But here I am. And now I have to find food and shelter. But I will make it. Just to prove to the universe that I am a winner."

Her voice was harsh, bitter, cold.

What happened to this poor girl?

"The universe is an inanimate object." It was the first thing Cheyenne could think of to reply to her.

"A higher power. Whatever."

"Are you talking about God? God is not an *it*."

Leila shrugged. "I don't believe in God."

"Because?"

"Isn't it obvious? If He exists, why am I suffering? Why?"

"Sin. Sin is why."

"Have I sinned? I didn't ask to be conceived. I didn't ask for my own father to abandon us. I didn't ask for my mother to hate me. I didn't ask for a sorry life." She began to cry softly.

Without a word, Cheyenne left her chair, went to the other side of the table, and wrapped her arms around Leila.

She wondered how many Leilas there are in the world, abandoned and unloved.

No family.

No shelter.

No food.

No money.

Lord Jesus, what do I say to her?

Suddenly, Leila pushed Cheyenne away. "Whatcha doing? I can't breathe."

"Oh sorry. I thought you needed a hug."

"Well, hug time is over." Leila dried her eyes. "Let me help you throw out the trash."

Cheyenne realized that Roger was unemotional like that too. Maybe this was really his daughter.

Still, they had to confirm it with a DNA test, and that had to happen sooner than later.

"Not before we have a piece of the delicious pound cake, loaded with sugar," Cheyenne said.

"Cake? I like cakes."

"We get free food every now and then. One of the residents of the housing division next door brought us this cake last night."

They ate quickly as Cheyenne kept glancing at her watch. Lunchtime was almost over for her.

"Are there jobs at the fire station?" Leila suddenly asked.

"Well, we could also use new firefighters, but it takes time for training."

Leila's shoulder's sagged. "I need a job like yesterday. Can I do dishes or something?"

"We take turns to cook and clean, so I don't think that's an option. We have some volunteers, but they're unpaid. Have you checked the restaurants in town?"

"Yes, this morning before you picked me up at the riverfront. I walked up and down River Street, looking for something. Anything."

"If you like, I can ask around at church to see. Restaurant jobs?"

"Yeah. I like the tips."

"Okay." Cheyenne thought of Jerome Pendegrast and his other riverboat, but she didn't want to say it right now. What if it didn't turn out? She decided she had better talk to Jerome first before she got Leila's hopes up.

"So do I need a GED to apply to be a firefighter?" Leila asked.

"Yeah. You need at least a high school diploma or GED. Some of the firefighters here have a college degree." Cheyenne collected their paper plates and plastic forks to take back inside the fire station recycling bins. "Then you have to go to school."

"To learn how to fight fires?"

"Uh huh."

"Okay. I'm not saying I want to be a firefighter."

"It's a great job, I can tell you. I love it. I get to help people all the time," Cheyenne said. "I've got some EMT training, and I might go that route, or I might want to be an arson investigator down the road. Lots of opportunities."

"Arson investigator?" Leila's eyes widened. "Like what I heard on the news? Did you ever catch the arsonist yet?"

"So you heard. Well, the local PD—police department—works on that, but yes, we help them in many ways. No, we haven't caught him or her. There might be more than one person."

"The news said it's been years."

"Terrible, isn't it?"

"You'd think they would've caught the criminals by now."

"Might be copycats at work too."

"Hope they don't hit restaurants because that's where I want to work," Leila said.

"We need all the help we can get to apprehend the criminals."

Leila did a mock salute. "I'm just doing my civic duty."

Cheyenne glanced at her watch. Her lunch hour is over. She had to go wash the truck next. So far, there had been no fires in twenty hours. But there was plenty to do around the station.

"Are you sure you don't need a ride to wherever you need to go?" Cheyenne asked.

"No. I'm handing out my resume to area businesses in person. I'm going to be in and out of stores in this area, and making my way back to the river."

"Where did you sleep last night?" Cheyenne asked again.

Leila didn't reply this time.

"You know it's going to rain tonight."

"How did you..."

"You said 'back to the river.' I made a guess."

Cheyenne pointed to Leila's oversized backpack. "And that. You can't miss that big bag."

"You should be an arson investigator."

Cheyenne laughed.

"Were there a lot of people at the park last night?"

"I don't know, to be honest. I got there late, and it was dark. I just found an empty spot and went to sleep. I heard snores all around me. Those kept me awake. I spent most of the night watching container ships go up and down the river, and looking at the lights across the river at that nice fancy hotel."

"Sounds like camping." Back in her college days, Cheyenne liked to camp, but not so much these days.

"It was camping. There's even a public restroom they don't lock."

"Where will you go tonight?" Cheyenne asked as they stood at the front of the fire station door.

"If I get a job, I could stay at the Y or get a room at a cheap motel."

Cheyenne had a suggestion for Leila, but she wasn't sure if Leila would agree to it.

"Do you want me to look for a place for you to stay?" Cheyenne asked.

"Where?"

"I don't know if they can take one more person, but I think I can pull some strings."

"This entire time we had lunch, you didn't say anything."

"Because I haven't asked them."

"Okay. So what is this place?"

"It's maybe ten minutes from here. It's a ministry run by a friend of a friend. If you're a homeless teen who needs a place to stay and do your laundry so you can finish school or get your GED, you can stay there until you graduate from high school or can afford to support yourself."

"What's the catch?" Leila's voice sounded harsh.

"I wanted to know too. My friend, Officer Garcia, says that they are a legitimate charitable organization."

"Your friend's a cop?"

Cheyenne nodded. "We go to the same church. The couple fostered a lot of children, and they started this ministry to help older teens."

"Homeless teens. Many of us?" Leila's voice softened.

"I don't know, but the couple running the ministry getting older, and they want my church to take over," Cheyenne explained. "That's all I know. It's a new project my church is praying about."

"And you want me to stay there?"

"I can't make you go, but I think that it's a safer

place than sleeping outside in a park with a bunch of strangers, you know?"

"I don't want handouts."

"Oh no. They want you to either finish high school or get your GED. They want you working. And it's only temporary."

"Temporary?" Leila sniffled. "Everything is temporary, isn't it? Like I might as well have never been born. Nobody cares, nobody wants, nobody nothing."

"God cares. God wants. God is everything."

Leila didn't reply.

"What do you think?" Cheyenne asked. "I don't know if they'll take you since you're eighteen, but I can ask, since you haven't finished high school."

"They have rules, I'm sure."

"Yeah. No cussing. No smoking. No alcohol. No drugs. No friends over. And they want you to attend church at least once a week."

Leila didn't flinch. "A clean place to stay, shower, sleep. I can handle church."

"You sure?" It was Cheyenne's turn to ask now.

"Yeah. Hopefully church people are better to me than people in the shelters or out in the streets."

Shelter?

Streets?

Cheyenne thought that Leila's face changed a bit, as if she realized she was in a bad state.

Only eighteen and homeless.

CHAPTER SEVENTEEN

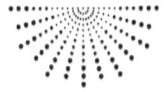

"That's going too far, Cheyenne." Roger was upset, and he knew it showed on his almost-forty face. He couldn't rein it in.

He knew no one could hear him talk to Cheyenne in his office at lunchtime, when all the able-bodied residents were next door at lunch in the SSLR dining room.

Yes, the door was ajar.

But Roger couldn't contain his frustration.

"You wanted me to talk with you before I do anything with my own life?" Cheyenne asked. She was standing by the window, arms crossed over her chest again.

It wasn't like she was hiding anything from him —except her own thoughts—but Roger wanted transparency from Cheyenne, perhaps a heads-up before she went and did this. Among other things, he didn't want to be liable for any fallout.

"You're doing me a favor," Roger explained. "I didn't ask for you to put yourself in danger."

"I make my own decisions."

"Yeah, but this involves me."

"I didn't volunteer you to provide her with room and board."

"You don't know if she's a criminal." His voice softened.

"It's not your house. And it's only for a few days until Sunrise Hill has a bed available. They told me they'd know by next week."

"I don't want her in your house."

"I'll lock my bedroom door at night."

"She'll be in your home."

"I do have a license to carry."

"Seriously? I had no idea." Roger couldn't believe what he was hearing.

"I was in the Army, remember? I know how to protect myself."

"But still... She'll be in your house. What if she turns out not to be Victorina? Not my daughter?" Quite instantly, Roger decided that he'd better call Ming again. It didn't matter how much it cost to run a complete investigation on Leila, possibly Victorina. Or whoever she might be in real life.

There was more at stake now. The stranger who

had come to town looking for what she had lost—or what she never had in the first place—had encroached on the life of someone Roger cared for.

Cared?

Yes, I care for Cheyenne.

Perhaps more than he had cared for other women lately. He had put her aside because he knew he was not good enough for her.

Not after all that he had done in his life.

No.

"I asked her to come to church with me on Sundays," Cheyenne said.

"What?"

"You missed that part, didn't you?"

"Ah..."

"I told you before that maybe she's in town because she needs Jesus."

"We all need Jesus. She doesn't have to be here in Savannah to need Jesus."

"But she is. Maybe God sent her here," Cheyenne added.

"We discussed all that. Spiritual side notwithstanding, I don't know who she is. I don't want you hurt." Roger was standing close enough to Cheyenne to reach for her hand.

Or chin.

He felt so helpless.

He needed Cheyenne's help to sort out his

problem with Leila. But not this kind of help. "It never crossed my mind that you would invite a homeless girl to stay with you."

"She will be safe in my home. Out there in the park, she's sleeping in the open. Who knows what sort of danger she could be in. She could catch a disease or get raped."

Roger flinched.

None of those things ever crossed his mind.

"Let me help her. If she is not your daughter, so be it. Maybe this is the only chance she has to encounter Jesus. If I don't help her, who will?"

Roger stepped toward her. "I'm sorry that I dragged you into this."

"I agreed to be a part of this."

"I don't know why you're still here, going the extra mile, when I have nothing to give you."

"I don't want anything in return. What are friends for?"

Friends? "I think of you as more than a friend."

"Me too, but you won't hear me say it." Cheyenne chuckled.

"No? Why?" Roger stepped closer.

He was close enough now to put his hand on her shoulder or waist.

He didn't know why he was drawn to Cheyenne.

But I am.

Was she also drawn to him? He had to find out.

She smelled like spring flowers. Maybe it's her shampoo or lotion or something. But the fresh breeze beckoned him to maybe run a finger through her hair.

Her pretty hair glistened in the noonday sun shining down on her at the tall window. Her eyes were bright and brown, the same color as her hair.

Roger studied her eyes again. No, they weren't brown, actually.

They looked more hazel.

Or something.

He had to take a closer look.

There were specks of green in her eyes.

Green?

Maybe greenish gold?

And her cheeks were smooth and soft, quite a contrast to the dry pads of his thumb. Maybe he could ask her what lotion she used that could make his hands softer so he didn't scratch her face when he ran his fingers along her jawline.

She didn't pull back or push him away. She stayed there, standing by the window with the pool of noonday light on her, like a spotlight of some sort.

She didn't feel nervous against him either. In fact, she seemed to welcome his touch.

Roger knew then that something was happening between them. His problems faded into the backseat as Cheyenne took center stage in his mind.

A respite from his troubles, past and present.

Her lips were smooth, soft, sweet, tasting like strawberries.

He wondered what lip gloss she used—

Honk!

Honk! Honk!

Roger's eyes snapped open, Cheyenne still in his arms.

"Oh dear." Cheyenne chuckled as she pointed out the window, where they had been standing.

And kissing.

There, on the path on the other side of the bed of flowers, was Miss Gemma in her pink wheelchair. In her hand was a bike horn.

A bike horn?

"I thought we confiscated that." Roger let go of Cheyenne.

Honk!

Honk! Honk!

Miss Gemma waved to them. Her mouth opened and shut, but Roger couldn't hear a word.

Apparently, Cheyenne could read her lips. "She wants to know—haha! No."

"What? What?" Roger asked.

"Nothing."

"Nothing what? She said something. Should I go out there to ask?"

"You better not."

"I have to deal with the noise ordinance." Roger let her go. "How many bike horns does your aunt have?"

"I only know of that one from the other day."

Roger looked out the window. Miss Gemma was still there. The octogenarian was puckering her lips and honking a horn that was so loud that Roger could hear it from this side of the closed window.

Roger opened the window and stuck his head out. "Miss Gemma, please stop honking. You know you're possessing an illegal contraband."

"I'll stop honking if you tell me when you're having a baby!"

Roger was so startled at what Miss Gemma said, that he bumped the back of his head hard on the window sill.

Behind him, Cheyenne could not stop laughing.

CHAPTER EIGHTEEN

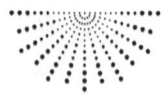

"Only until Monday morning, okay?" Cheyenne asked as she invited Leila into her townhouse.

It was only Thursday.

Cheyenne would be home tonight, but her twenty-four-hour shift started again on Friday. She'd have to leave Leila alone until Saturday night, when she had her forty-eight-hour break from work.

Alone.

A stranger in her townhouse.

"Are you having second thoughts?" Leila lowered her backpack at the front door. She was still standing outside.

"If you want me to sign something about what we agreed on, I can do that," Leila said. "We should do that before I step into your house."

"I don't think that's necessary."

"We agreed that I'll be here from today, Thursday, until Monday morning. You said Mrs. Hill would let us know Sunday at church whether I have a room for Monday night."

And if not?

Roger was right. This was a bad idea.

Cheyenne prayed quickly for after-the-fact wisdom from God.

"You also know that I have started studying for my GED," Leila pleaded her case. "I am determined to at least get that one done. Then I can get a full-time job or go to college."

Cheyenne prayed quietly for wisdom.

It was too late to backtrack now. She was in too deep.

It had all begun with trying to get Leila a safe place to sleep at night. When there had been a delay at Sunrise Hill...

What overcame me?

"What else do you need from me?" Leila asked.

"How about the truth of why you're here in Savannah?"

"I told you, right? I'm looking for my biological father. Apparently one of five men is my real father."

"How are you going about doing that?"

"Obviously we're all going to take DNA tests."

Cheyenne nodded. "Costly."

"They're going to pay for theirs. I will pay for mine."

"How many have you contacted?"

"Three. Two left. One might be deceased. I'm in Savannah for the last one." Leila sighed. "Now you know the whole truth."

Cheyenne truly had no idea what she was getting herself into.

Yeah, a favor.

Then again, this was more than returning a favor.

Cheyenne stood there, inside her foyer, while Leila stayed on the other side of her door.

They had come too far for Cheyenne to send Leila away.

Leila had said she was eighteen, but she looked no more than sixteen.

There were bags under her sad eyes.

"Forget it." Leila picked up her backpack. "I don't need your pity. I don't need anyone's pity."

She turned to go.

Just as a sense of relief swept over Cheyenne, a sense of guilt slapped her in her face.

She had been trying to help this homeless girl—who could be Roger's daughter.

Even if she wasn't, she was still a homeless girl in need of Christ.

And it would only be for four nights.

What could possibly happen in four nights?

Maybe she could ask a friend for help. Maybe someone from church she trusted, like Officer Corazon Garcia.

Cheyenne knew that Cora also worked in shifts at the Savannah-Chatham Metropolitan Police Department. If she could just stop by at random hours to check on Leila, maybe it would all work out.

Oh, but to burden another person.

I wish I'd never offered this stranger a place to stay.

Then again...

The poor homeless teenager!

Cheyenne went after Leila. "I'm sorry."

"You have nothing to be sorry about. I'm a stranger. I wouldn't invite me in either." Leila adjusted her backpack over her shoulders.

"I'm truly sorry," Cheyenne repeated. "The honest truth is that I have no idea what I am getting into. I want to help you, but I don't know you."

"We're strangers. You don't know if you could get rid of me on Monday morning."

"Then again..."

"What?"

"God might have brought you here for such a time as this to meet Jesus Christ."

"Meet Jesus? I don't want to die."

Cheyenne chuckled. "Looks like there's a lot to explain, but life and death are in God's hands. What I am trying to say is that we didn't meet at the restaurant for nothing. I believe that God is sovereign and He has a beautiful plan for your life."

Leila sniffled. "God doesn't care."

"Yes, He does. He sustained you all these years, hasn't He?"

Leila shrugged. "I don't know."

"He brought you here."

"I came to town on a bus."

"Well, God directed you here."

"I made the decision myself," Leila insisted. "I want to know where I came from."

"Who are you? Why are you here? Where are you going?"

Leila nodded. "Basic questions of life that I have no answer to."

"To me, the answer belongs to God."

"To you."

"Yes, to me."

CHAPTER NINETEEN

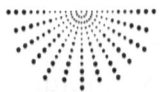

*T*here she was, sitting on the bench outside his office, staring at him as he walked down the hallway.

Leila Somebody.

Roger knew this day would come. He just knew it.

However, he hadn't expected it to be this soon. He had been thinking that she'd show up next week sometime, after she had settled down at the home for teens or gotten a new job somewhere in town.

Yet, there she was.

No, he wasn't afraid of her.

Not at all.

Surprised didn't describe Roger at this moment in time, these few minutes before lunchtime at SSLR.

Relieved was the word.

Sheer relief.

Roger's past had finally caught up with him.

In many ways, he was glad that he could finally face his many sins and put them behind him.

Perhaps.

Sins have consequences.

A reminder all too painful to him these days.

The girl didn't move from where she sat.

And she was still staring at him.

Daring him to keep walking toward her?

Roger gulped.

Maybe I'm not as brave as I thought.

His feet didn't get the memo. They kept walking, his Louis Vitton loafers tapped softly on the polished floor.

When he came face to face with the girl, he stopped.

And said nothing.

She also said nothing.

Time, on the other hand, said a lot.

The poor girl looked tired, more so than the first time Roger had seen her at Piper's Place, serving tables. He knew that she had been homeless, and that Cheyenne—bless her heart!—had given her a place to stay until Sunrise Hill had a vacancy.

Speaking of Cheyenne, Roger wondered if she knew that Leila was here.

He couldn't remember when Cheyenne had to be at the fire station for her shift. He usually texted her and if she responded, she responded. Otherwise, Roger didn't ask what her schedule was.

Now, at this moment, standing in front of a potential blast from his past, all Roger could think of was Cheyenne and where she was.

Cheyenne would know how to handle this situation.

"Do you remember me?" the girl asked.

"You're the server at Piper's Place." Roger was grateful she had spoken first.

"Was. I no longer work there, but I've got an interview this afternoon." She stared at him.

He stared back. "How did you get in here?"

"Walked in through a gate," Leila said.

"Walked through or climbed over?"

"Through." Leila motioned her hand like it was a fish. "The side gate in the back where they drop off groceries."

"Huh."

"It must be the back of the kitchen, right?"

"Didn't security stop you?" Roger had put security at the main gate, but there should be a truck patrolling the grounds.

Most of the time, it was to prevent SSLR residents from wandering off the property. Sometimes residents with Alzheimer's forgot where they lived.

"There was no security there," Leila replied. "A grocery truck was leaving, so I walked in as the gate opened."

"And no one stopped you." Roger made a mental note to beef up security.

Leila tilted her head. "I'm not looking for charity."

"What is your real name?" Roger asked.

"You might as well know." She blinked a few times. "I'm Victorina Mays."

More relief coursed through Roger's heart.

It's all out in the open now.

What's left is a DNA test. Or two DNA tests.

"No middle name?" Roger had no idea why he wanted to know.

She shook her head. "I gave myself one. Leila."

"Why didn't your mother give you a middle name?"

"She's generous that way. Hold something back for leverage. But you knew that." Leila looked at Roger.

Roger remained stoic. "I wouldn't know."

Not only did he not want to badmouth the mother of his potential daughter, he had no idea if anything he said would work against him later.

This here girl might be a con artist.

"Why are you here?" Roger continued his questioning.

"I have to know. Don't you?"

Roger folded his arms. "You couldn't have asked me the first day we met at Piper's Place?"

"I had to work up some courage."

"How did you know I was going to be there that night anyway?"

Leila sat back on the bench, looking a bit more relaxed. Or not. "Well, I didn't know. I googled you and found out that you work here. I also found out you attend Riverside Chapel. Then I found out the church members there like to eat at Piper's Place."

"How so?"

"There was a local news article about the restaurant owner, and she talked about her church and Sunday lunches."

"Ah."

"So I put two and two together, and hoped that you'd be among those who eat at Piper's Place." Leila waved her hands. "You didn't show for two weeks."

"Well, I don't eat there all the time."

"It was nice that you finally did."

Roger was glad he didn't see any tattoos on her bare arms. In fact, Leila wore no jewelry at all.

"But that Tuesday night, though," Roger pressed.

"Well, I worked there weekends and weeknights. I figured that since you work during the day, you're more likely to show up at Piper's at night."

"If at all."

"Piper said that church members get discounts if they bring their church bulletins."

"You imagined I might take advantage of that."

"Since your work bio doesn't say you're married," Leila said. "Unless, of course, you cook at home."

"Which I do not."

"Fifty-fifty chance you might." Leila cleared her throat. "Did Mom tell you I'm in town?"

Roger didn't reply.

"I talked to her last night and she said she called you."

"What's your mother's name?"

Leila sighed. "You still don't believe me."

"What do you want?" Immediately, Roger knew it was the wrong question.

"I want us to take DNA tests. I can't afford mine, but I was hoping you would pay for mine. If you're not my father, then I will cross you off the list, and you will never see me again. I have four more potential candidates to ask, and they all live in different states across the country."

"What a mess," Roger said.

"Tell me about it. You didn't have to live with it for eighteen years, wondering who your father is."

"At least you have a mother. Some people don't have parents."

"And they're worse off?" Leila's eyes widened. "You don't know my mother, do you? She yelled at me on the phone last night. She's still mad I left home, but only because her other kids have no babysitter."

"Oh." Roger's heart felt heavy.

"I shouldn't have called her, but I did because I knew she'd be worried. I was right. She was worried, sure. But not for me."

Roger decided to stay out of it.

If he suggested that Mimi Mays was concerned about Leila a.k.a. Victorina, he would regret it. He didn't know enough to make a judgment on a woman he hadn't been with in nineteen years.

"What's next for you?" Roger asked.

"Regardless of the DNA test results, I'm on my own now." Leila's voice softened.

Roger felt something on his shoulder. A hand.

He turned to find Cheyenne standing next to him, wearing a tee shirt, jeans, and sandals. She placed a fluorescent green bike horn in Roger's hand.

"Oh no. Another one?" Roger frowned. "How many did your aunt buy?"

"I got her to confess. Three dozen on sale for forty percent off. A bargain, she said."

"No way. And where has she stashed them?" Roger could just imagine what would happen if Miss Gemma distributed those bike horns to other residents.

"I don't know." Cheyenne shrugged. "Hello, Leila. Did you sleep well last night?"

"Yes, thank you. First comfortable bed I've had since—uh." She paused for the longest time. "Hope I didn't wake you up this morning."

"You got up super early this morning," Cheyenne said. "I was going to make you breakfast."

"Thank you, but I didn't want to impose. I had some job leads. Wanted to be first in line."

"I'll keep praying for you that you'll get a good job."

"Thanks, I guess."

Roger missed Leila's facial expression in response to what Cheyenne said. He hoped that Leila's exposure to Christians would improve her view of Jesus Christ.

Especially since he himself was a poor example of a Christian.

Leila stood up hastily. "I better go."

Cheyenne stopped her. "Would you like to have lunch here? I'm sure that Roger could give us two lunch passes."

Roger glanced at Cheyenne, suddenly forgetting

that he had promised to pay for all meals in this project.

"S-sure." He pointed to his office. "Let me get you the meal tickets."

"I don't know," Leila said. "I don't want to be a burden."

Burden?

Roger wasn't sure what to think about that. "Have you had lunch?"

"No," Leila said.

"If you don't want to eat in the cafeteria, we could bag our lunches and eat in the garden—if that's all right with Roger." Cheyenne waited for him to say something.

"If I give you meal tickets, you're a guest. Just don't litter the gardens. Don't wander too far off, and don't fall into the ocean."

Leila laughed. Then straightened up. "Wait. What? Ocean? There's an ocean in the backyard?"

"It's not a backyard, but yes, the property goes up to the dunes," Roger said. "You can't mess with the dunes, but you can take the boardwalk all the way to the beach."

Cheyenne glanced at her watch. "I have half an hour to eat, and then I need to get to work."

"Got to catch the arsonist," Leila said.

Roger thought she seemed comfortable talking with Cheyenne.

"Maybe I can catch a ride with you back to Savannah," Leila said. "I need to look for work downtown, where it's more touristy. Get more tips in the restaurants there."

"Of course." Cheyenne looked at Roger. "Well, the sooner we get to lunch, the sooner we can get off the island."

"Right." Roger disappeared into his office, and returned with a couple of meal tickets and his business card. He handed the meal tickets to Cheyenne and his card to Leila.

"I'll call some doctors to find out where and when we can take reliable DNA tests," Roger said. "Next week, I only have two days to spare before my conference. What's a good day for you next week?"

"Until I find a job, any day." Leila studied Roger's business card. "You sound calm, Mr. Patel."

Roger didn't try to correct her. What could she call him? She might not be his daughter. There was only one in five chances than she was.

That was, assuming Mimi Mays hadn't slept with more than five men during that window so long ago.

Roger cringed even as the thought crossed his mind.

"Not so calm now." Cheyenne chuckled.

Roger waved them off. "I better get back to work."

"No lunch for you?" Cheyenne asked.

"I'll eat at my desk. Have to catch up on work."

Leila gasped. "Sorry that I interrupted your work."

What? A teenager apologizing?

Leila seemed genuinely apologetic.

Then again, she was eighteen. Didn't that make her legally an adult?

To Roger, if kids could be dependent on their parents for health insurance until they turned twenty-six years old, then that changed when they became adults, didn't it?

It was odd to him that an eighteen-year-old American could serve in the military, but they could not buy alcohol until they were twenty-one, and could stay on their parents' health care plan for five more years after that.

Whoa.

The thought hit him for real now.

I could be the father of an eighteen-year-old girl.

Whoa. I need to sit down.

"Roger?" Cheyenne crinkled her eyebrows. "Are you okay?"

"Wh—yeah." Roger snapped into the moment. "I better eat something. I'll walk you ladies to the dining hall and then we can go our separate ways."

Even as he said it, he wished he hadn't offered.

CHAPTER TWENTY

"*I* think you're worrying unnecessarily."

Diego Flores dipped the breaded shrimp into the chili sauce.

Roger watched his pastor enjoy the shrimp without a care in the world. He leaned back on the deck chair, closed his eyes, and chewed slowly.

Roger looked at the bowl of shrimp and dip that he had bought for them. Half the shrimp was gone.

He turned to gaze across the beach and the Atlantic Ocean, to the sky in sunset colors. The sun was setting behind the Flores's beach house, so they couldn't see it go down. But the sky was washed in hues of coral and red and shades of blue here and there.

On a normal day, Roger would have taken a photograph with his iPhone. Usually, he would be sitting on the deck on the second floor of his own beach house, only five minutes from here.

And he would be on his own deck chair, without a care in the world.

Not today.

Right now, having skipped dinner, he didn't feel like eating the expensive shrimp he had brought for Diego. He was still digesting that roast beef sandwich he had for lunch. And the bags of potato chips he had binged on after Cheyenne and Leila had left.

They sat in silence for a good bit.

Roger listened to the ocean waves.

Just waiting for his old friend Diego to put on his preaching hat and become Pastor Diego Flores.

He didn't have to wait long.

"The Christian life is not meant to be convenient, but cleansing," Diego said, eyes still closed.

"Am I being cleansed now?" Roger asked.

"You've heard Christians say before that God allows what He allows."

"To discipline me? To punish me? To prove a point?"

Diego opened his eyes. "God loves you and will only allow what's best for you."

"Even if it's a mess of my own doing."

"God can make all things new." Diego sat up. "What do you think about Isaiah 42:9?"

Behold, the former things have come to pass,
   And new things I declare;
   Before they spring forth I tell you of them.

"That verse reminds me of that other Isaiah verse about streams in the desert." Roger didn't wait for Diego to ask him to look it up. He swiped his iPhone and did the honors. "Here it is. Isaiah 35:6b."

For waters shall burst forth in the wilderness,
   And streams in the desert.

"It's a good verse." Diego ate more shrimp.

"Thank you for meeting with me this Friday evening, when you should really be out on a date with your wife," Roger said.

"Date? We date every evening—dinner together, walk on the beach together, read together, pray together. Plenty of date nights."

"That must be nice to have someone to share life with."

"So says a bachelor." Diego smiled.

Bachelor.

Roger wondered if he wanted to remain a bachelor. That idea had gone on well until he went out with Cheyenne—

Went out? What?

She was only returning a favor.

It probably meant more to him than to her. She had nothing to lose. Leila was not Cheyenne's daughter.

Once the project was over, Cheyenne could go back to her normal life.

Roger would still be stuck with a daughter—if the DNA results panned out.

"When do you find out?" Diego asked.

"We haven't taken the DNA test yet. We'll go to the lab separately next week. It has to be Monday or Tuesday, since I'm flying out to a conference on Tuesday night."

As soon as Roger had returned to his desk with his lunch that afternoon, he called around and found walk-in labs for paternity tests.

"If she is your daughter?" Diego asked.

"I have to tell our church, or at least my Sunday School class." Roger didn't know if they would understand.

"Spiritually mature Christians won't cast the first stone."

"I may need to take a break from teaching. I need to get my own life straightened out."

Diego nodded. "Pray about it and see where God leads. His ways are always the best, but we both already knew that."

Dusk fell above the deck, covering Tybee Island like a shroud.

Diego pointed to the rest of the shrimp on the tray between their two deck chairs.

"You eat them up," Roger said. "I'll eat something later when I get home."

"No appetite, huh?" Diego reached for the shrimp on the rickety side table.

"One way to lose weight, for sure." Roger patted his tummy.

The clouds and stars played hide-and-seek in the sky. Roger didn't want to go home to an empty beach house, a meaningless opulence to him now.

He'd be happy in this little old cottage that Diego and Heidi owned. Small, comfortable, homey.

Roger's own beach house had walls of cold windows. Maybe he could renovate it and add more wood.

Nah. He didn't need another project to distract himself from his problems.

"I need the peace of Christ that surpasses all comprehension or understanding," Roger declared.

"Because you're saved, you have Jesus, the prince of peace."

"But, I sinned with Mimi against God in my early days of Christianity. I don't have the "before card" that said the sin was committed before I got saved. How could I have fallen that far?"

"Back in the old days, you would have to marry the girl you impregnate." Diego often sprinkled such trivia throughout his sermons. "Today, if you force a marriage, it could very well end in divorce, and you'd be back to where you started."

"However, the baby—child—would not be born out of wedlock."

"For how long?" Diego asked. "Did you think you would have been happily married to Leila's mother?"

Roger didn't have to take long to think about the answer. "No. She and I were not in love. We were in med school. May I speak freely?"

"No one is listening but we and God."

"She and I were relieving stress, I think. Med school was hard, and we were on the verge of flunking out. Mimi dropped out soon afterwards." Roger didn't have to repeat the rest of the story that Diego knew. "At least we didn't take drugs or become alcoholics."

Diego lifted a finger. "A sin by any measure is still a sin. One sin is all it takes to send you to the infernal place. Doesn't matter how big or small."

Roger nodded. "You're right. I have asked God to forgive me so many times."

"Do you believe He has forgiven you?"

"Yes. I got 1 John 1:9 memorized."

If we confess our sins, He is faithful and just to forgive us our sins and to cleanse us from all unrighteousness.

"If you have asked God to forgive you of your sins, and He has done so through Jesus Christ, why are you still not feeling forgiven?" Diego asked.

"Shouldn't I be asking you that question?"

"You know the answer."

"It's not about feelings."

"Yes, that too. It's about faith and not feeling, but there's something else."

Roger thought about it for a good bit. "What?"

"You haven't forgiven yourself."

"It's a big mess."

"Forgiving yourself doesn't mean that you have to run to your ex-girlfriend, marry her, and raise her children," Diego said. "Forgiveness doesn't necessarily demand reconciliation."

"What about sowing and reaping?"

"That's another verse altogether. Do you see the word *forgive* in that verse?"

Roger read Galatians 6:7-8 from his Bible app.

Do not be deceived, God is not mocked; for whatever a man sows, that he will also reap. For he who sows to his flesh will of the flesh reap corruption, but he who sows to the Spirit will of the Spirit reap everlasting life.

"Even if you're forgiven, you still have to face the consequences of your action," Diego said.

That was all his friend needed to say. Roger knew what he had to do: forgive himself for the guilt of his own sins, but also deal with the fallout of his old sins.

CHAPTER TWENTY-ONE

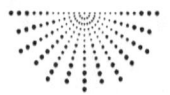

*R*oger had missed Sunday School this morning. Cheyenne had found out from Ming, who was in Roger's class. She hoped Roger wasn't planning on skipping church altogether. That would be an odd behavior coming from Roger, who was always at church ever since Cheyenne had moved to Savannah.

In between Sunday School and the church service, Cheyenne saved two other seats in the dining room, where Riverside Chapel had held its services for some years. She sat down in the third chair, and looked around, but did not see Leila anywhere.

Leila had gone to the college Sunday School class instead of staying with Cheyenne in the singles class. Cheyenne was still surprised that Leila had agreed to go to Sunday School on top of the church service. Granted, Cheyenne provided the only transportation, and attending church was part of their room-and-board agreement—although Cheyenne prayed that it would not turn Leila against Christ.

No, Leila agreed to come with me to church.

For one Sunday only.

Leila found her. "You saved me a seat? Thank you so much."

"You look happy. Did your college Sunday School class go well?" Cheyenne asked.

"Yes, very well." Leila sat down. "On the way here, I ran into the pastor's wife. Said she knows I'm looking for a job, and she gave me some information."

"Yeah? Where?"

"At the University of Coastal Georgia, where she works. The cafeteria hires all the time, but two people are out on maternity leave, so maybe I could help in the kitchen."

The piano began to play, and Cheyenne quietly thanked God for Leila's job leads.

Well into the opening prayer, Roger still hadn't shown up.

After they sang a few more hymns, Cheyenne texted Roger, telling him that she was waiting for him.

A minute later, he texted back, saying that he was looking for a parking spot.

It was a good thing that Cheyenne had saved him a seat.

~

*R*oger rarely missed Sunday School. Unless he was sick or church was closed or he was out of town, Roger would automatically be at church for all events and services.

But.

Today, shame had shackled him to his house.

He prayed at home during the Sunday School hour.

Ah. Pious pity.

Now his shame had multiplied. He would be walking into the service late—although Diego hadn't started preaching yet—in front of everyone.

It was entirely possible that nobody was looking at him.

However, Roger felt self-conscious.

Am I only trying to punish myself for my shameful past?

Hasn't Jesus nailed all my sins to His cross? All my sins?

All of them?

He double-stepped up the ramp, and quietly entered the dining room.

Diego was at the pulpit, opening his Bible. He seemed to be waiting for everyone to settle down.

Roger picked up the morning program, and looked for the table where Cheyenne said she had saved him a seat.

To her credit, her table was at the very back.

He quickly sat down.

Cheyenne smiled.

Roger didn't want to sit with Cheyenne. People would talk.

About what?

"Today we're going to start a new series on God's mercy," Diego said from the pulpit. "Open with me to the book of Jude."

As Roger opened his Bible, he glanced over to Leila, sitting on the other side of Cheyenne.

Leila had a Bible. Good.

Roger whispered to Cheyenne to help Leila find Jude in the New Testament.

"I was going to," Cheyenne whispered back.

At that moment, Roger wanted to give Cheyenne a hug.

But he didn't.

CHAPTER TWENTY-TWO

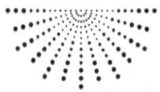

"This is a change," Leila announced as she looked at the Piper's Place lunch menu. "The last time I was here, I was serving. Today, I'm being served."

She sat next to Cheyenne on the other side of the table from Roger. He was able to see both of them together.

It made him a bit uncomfortable.

If Cheyenne were the only person across from the table, then Roger would feel at home. They had been friends for three years.

Leila was new to his life. Yes, he knew she existed, but now she was here in Savannah, right in front of him.

On Monday, they'd both go to the lab to get their DNA taken for paternity testing.

Right now, after church on Sunday, here they were, in limbo.

To Roger, Leila was still a child. She might be eighteen years old, but she had grown up in a broken home and had missed a lot of normal child-hood—or what Roger would consider a carefree childhood.

Yes, she was a child.

Struggling on her own through life.

After the server came and took their orders, everyone sipped cold water. For some reason, no one ordered tea or soda.

"Are you going to college?" Roger asked Leila.

"What?" Leila seemed to have been lost in some thought.

"College?" Roger repeated.

"I need my GED first, don't I?" Leila asked.

"And after that?"

"I don't know."

"What are your plans for the next five years?"

"Don't know." Leila frowned. "Why are you asking me stuff like that?"

Cheyenne didn't say a word.

Everyone waited for Roger to say whatever.

Roger felt that he had started it, so he might as well bring the whole conversation to some sort of conclusion.

"You're young," Roger began. "You have a whole

life ahead of you. Don't mess up like some people have."

"Like you have?"

"We may or may not be related, but I am old enough to advise you not to waste the precious time God has given you."

"Don't give me the God card." Leila sat back. "Where were you when I was five or six and starving?"

"Why were you starving? Five men sent your mother money."

"Where was the money?"

"Maybe you could ask your mother," Roger said.

Cheyenne put her hands up. "You two, we're trying to have a peaceful lunch here. How about we just talk about family issues later and just enjoy our meal?"

Roger felt chastised. "You're right, Cheyenne. I'm sorry."

He glanced over to find Leila moved by what he just said.

Was it because he told Cheyenne he was sorry?

He might never know because Leila didn't say a word.

He didn't want to say anything more himself, lest he caused more trouble than he had already created for everyone.

He wondered what Cheyenne thought of him.

Sure, he remembered how understanding she had been when he first told her about his fatherhood. What if she had been in shock at that time?

What about now?

What does she think of me now?

Cheyenne sat there quietly, sipping her glass of water.

Roger chided himself for having kissed her several days before. Why had he done that?

Does she know I meant it?

She had not protested. They would have kissed longer had Miss Gemma not interrupted them outside his office window.

However, he had been wrong to kiss her in his office.

Now every time he walked into his office, he remembered their kiss.

If she had been his wife, it wouldn't have been a big deal because he would be expected to kiss his beloved.

I must tell her I'm serious.

The next time they were alone, Roger would ask her if she had a new boyfriend.

Would that be the wrong question?

Before he could consider the options and make a flow chart of the ramifications, their salad came.

"Would you like to say grace for us?" Roger asked Cheyenne.

Cheyenne nodded. "Dear Lord Jesus, thank you for church this morning and for this delicious lunch. I pray that Your perfect will would prevail in every area of our lives—physically, emotionally, mentally, and spiritually. I pray that You will reveal the truth to Leila and Roger regarding their...um, situation. I pray that You will give us wisdom regarding our continuing education, careers, and future. Again, for the food, please provide nourishment for our bodies that we may serve You without shame. In Jesus' Name I pray. Amen."

Serve You without shame.

Roger wondered what Cheyenne meant by that.

One more thing to ask her later.

CHAPTER TWENTY-THREE

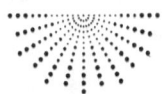

*C*heyenne was more than surprised when the multicolored bouquet of flowers arrived at the fire station. It was the worst place on earth for Roger to send them.

Sure enough, everyone teased her endlessly on the two calls they had that night.

That's right. Two calls in one night.

Oddly enough, no one questioned the fact that there were two fires that night within minutes of each other.

All her team members wanted to know was why Dr. Roger Patel had sent Cheyenne flowers.

Of course, Owen filled in all the blanks for her.

The teasing went on all afternoon, all evening, and into the night until a two-block fire interrupted them.

Now they were going back to the fire station.

Cheyenne looked out the window of the fire truck—tired, exhausted, and smelling like smoke. It was five in the morning, and she hadn't slept all night.

She wondered what time Roger got up in the morning. Would he be reading his Bible first thing? Would he still continue to be hard on himself for his past mistakes? Past sins?

Cheyenne could not recall committing any such sin in her own life. It must be hard on Roger to have fathered a child, paid for child support, and then have the child show up at his doorstep.

I don't know.

Never had to experience such a thing.

"Whatcha thinking about?" Owen was at the wheel, making their last turn down the street.

Around them, firefighters—thick with the smell of smoky sweat—were dozing off.

Cheyenne straightened up in her seat, adjusted the safety belt, and shook her head. "I just need to lie down right now."

"Same here." Owen smiled.

He had a brotherly smile, Cheyenne thought. With a smile like that, and a bright personality, why couldn't Owen get a date for months? He had tried some internet Christian dating service, which horrified Cheyenne when she had first heard of it.

Then again, she wouldn't want to do to Owen what he had done to her—and get him a blind date with the woman he had been pining after.

Well, Cora is single...

Cheyenne stopped herself. Even though Officer Corazon Garcia and Owen were about the same age, Cheyenne should not interfere.

Let God handle this.

If Cora and Owen were meant to be together, it would eventually happen, wouldn't it?

"Say, why did Roger send you those flowers?" Owen asked as he backed up the fire truck into the fire station.

Cheyenne shrugged.

"There was no message beyond the *to* and *from*."

He noticed.

"I think he's just being grateful. I helped him with his daughter," Cheyenne guessed.

Yeah. Why didn't Roger leave a note of some sort?

"So call him and ask him what the flowers are for." Owen could be pushy if he wanted to.

Maybe that's why he doesn't have a girlfriend right now.

"He's at a geriatric conference. Priyanka was supposed to go, but she developed morning sickness or something. So she's holding down the SSLR fort, and Roger has gone in her place."

Owen grinned. "So you're in the know."

"Know what?" Cheyenne was outside the fire truck.

"You know his schedule."

"Only because of his daughter."

"That so?"

"That's all, Owen. Don't read too much into a gesture of kindness."

Flowers, though.

In the three years Cheyenne had known Roger, she had never received flowers from him. Miss Gemma had never mentioned Roger sending flowers to anyone.

His cousin had been the one to persuade him to plant a patch of daffodils. According to Miss Gemma, if it had been up to Roger, most of the outdoor landscape would be green and low maintenance.

Suddenly, Roger had sent Cheyenne flowers.

Ah, maybe I don't know him that well, after all.

Outside the fire station, it was still dark. Dawn hadn't broken. Cheyenne took in the cool breeze.

While she had her eyes closed, the fire alarm went off again.

CHAPTER TWENTY-FOUR

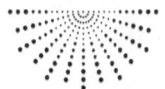

*I*t had been less than a week since Roger sent Cheyenne those flowers. He was out of town now, and unable to explain to her in person why he had sent her the bouquet. It must be puzzling to her, but Roger hoped that her work kept her too busy to think about it—that was, until he was able to get to her.

Out of town now for a conference, all that had to wait.

Roger entered the auditorium and sat in the back. Before he could take his conference folder out of his messenger bag, his phone buzzed.

Not now.

This was an all-important geriatrics roundtable, with an opportunity to have lunch with several rich donors afterwards.

Still, his phone buzzed.

Roger sighed.

As soon as he saw the text message, Roger bolted out of the conference room in seconds.

He rushed to an empty bench, sat down, drew a deep breath, and reread the message.

He called his cousin.

"What?" It was all he could say when Priyanka answered her phone.

"We sedated Miss Gemma," Priyanka said. "She's going to be all right."

"I don't care about her—I mean, I do, but I want to know what happened to Cheyenne again?" Roger found himself unable to breathe.

This can't be happening. We're just friends. Why am I caring so much?

"All I know is that both Owen and Cheyenne are at the hospital. Since we're not family, we're not getting a lot of details. Miss Gemma spoke to them, but since then, she has been incoherent all morning."

Roger drew a deep breath. "When was this?"

"A few hours ago."

"And it took you this long to text me?" Roger blurted.

"You were in the morning session. You did not want to be interrupted."

"I so want to be interrupted when it comes to Cheyenne—uh..."

Silence on the other end.

"What's going on between you two?" Priyanka finally asked.

"I—uh, I don't know." *That's the truth.*

"I'm waiting for Cheyenne's supervisor to call me back," Priyanka said. "I'd go to the hospital if I could, but I get dizzy in the car. If you hadn't let me stay here at SSLR, I wouldn't have been able to come to work every morning."

Roger felt selfish.

So selfish.

"I'm sorry, Pri. I forgot you have morning sickness and motion sickness."

"And everything else. Don't mention it. Nothing for you to apologize about."

"I'm still sorry. Cheyenne is not your concern."

"Miss Gemma is."

"Right. I'll call a few friends at Savannah Memorial to get some updates."

"I got some news googling, but they're not saying much. Something about an arsonist."

An arsonist. The one they'd been trying to catch for years, since Tamsyn's old house burned down.

Roger paced the hallway outside the conference room. "I wish I had prayed for her safety, you know."

"God knows His own," Priyanka said. "We can pray for them now."

"Yes, let's do." But Roger couldn't pray. In fact, he couldn't slow down his heart rate.

After Priyanka prayed a brief prayer, Roger barely said *amen*.

"Thanks for taking care of things at SSLR," Roger said.

"Don't mention it. I get paid to do this."

"I'll call a few friends. Tell Miss Gemma that everything will be all right."

"Will do when she comes around."

After Roger hung up, he lost interest in the entire conference.

His watch said it was almost eleven o'clock in Memphis. Savannah was one hour ahead. If he took a flight out by noon, he'd be back in Savannah before five.

It would cost him a fortune to change his flight from Friday night to right now, but he had to go to Cheyenne.

Have to?

Yeah, but I don't know why.

The question of the moment was: could he pack his bags in ten minutes?

CHAPTER TWENTY-FIVE

*R*oger floored the gas pedal, ran a yellow light, and ended up parked for a full five minutes outside Cheyenne's townhouse, unable to think or pray or get out of his SUV.

It had cost him hundreds of dollars to get a last-minute flight out of Memphis. His brother-in-law had picked him up from the Savannah/Hilton Head International Airport after work, and dropped him off at his house so he could get his SUV.

Half an hour later, here he was.

He took a deep breath, wondering what had overcome him.

It had freaked him out five ways to Christmas when he found out that Cheyenne had checked out of the hospital. Owen was still in the operating room for more surgeries on his back and legs, but Cheyenne had gone home.

By herself.

Someone should be driving her home.

Why is Cheyenne always so independent?

Roger glanced out the side window. He had never been to Cheyenne's house. But there was always a first time.

He exited his vehicle, locked the door, and walked slowly toward Cheyenne's front entrance.

There was a well-watered rosemary bush in a flower pot next to the doorbell. The worn doormat looked like it was made of coconut husks.

Now where on earth would Cheyenne have gotten a doormat like that?

Roger wondered what else didn't he know about her.

He rang the doorbell, and waited for what felt like a long time.

He didn't hear anything from the other side of the door, until it suddenly unlocked and opened.

"Roger?" Cheyenne sounded surprised to see him.

Roger stared.

Standing there in a tee shirt and a pair of jeans, Cheyenne was beautiful without any makeup, her dark brown hair softly cascading over her shoulders. She usually tied up her hair or kept it off her face, even at church, but today, she had let her hair down. Roger wondered if she hadn't tied up her hair because she only had one usable arm at this time.

Should he offer to do her hair?

What did just ask to do?

When Cheyenne stepped forward into the late afternoon sunlight, Roger saw that her entire left arm was in a cast, there was a big bruise on her forehead and several butterfly bandages on her chin and and jaw areas.

"Wh-what happened to you?" Roger asked. "I heard bits and pieces from everyone. So many conflicting news reports."

"Broke my arm in two places. It'll heal, and the cast will be off in less than two months. Aren't you supposed to be in Memphis?"

"I got home an hour ago," Roger said, "I... Well, I heard that you were in a terrible fire last night and I had to make sure you're fine."

"You're worried about me? Then pray, right?"

"I did."

"Good. God protected us. No one died. Only Owen is the most seriously injured. But Memphis, Roger. I thought your conference started this morning."

"I can always go back next year."

"But doesn't it cost a lot of money for hotel and flight and whatever?"

Not as costly as losing you.

"I'll reimburse SSLR for it."

"Out of pocket?"

Roger nodded. He couldn't wait to talk about Cheyenne instead of himself. "Are you all right?"

"Yeah. Thank God," Cheyenne said. "I would invite you inside, but I live alone, and I don't think it's a good idea for us to be behind closed doors, just the two of us."

"What?" Roger's eyebrows shot up.

Hadn't they kissed the other day in his office?

Why was Cheyenne suddenly cautious about their being together now?

"Why are you here, Roger?" Cheyenne tried again. "Truly?"

"I got a bit wor—concerned."

"Thank you for your concern. Like I said, God kept us all alive. In fact, Owen saved my life. He pushed me to firmer ground, but he lost his balance when the stairs crumbled, and he fell one floor down to the basement."

Roger was impressed that Cheyenne sounded clinical about it. She basically told him what had happened, without losing her cool or freaking out. Granted, she was a firefighter, but it had been a traumatic experience.

"Thank God that you and Owen survived," Roger said.

"He's going to need more surgeries to repair his back. When he hit the basement cement floor, he shattered bones. He may never walk again."

"But he's alive."

Cheyenne nodded. "Thing is, his parents are thousands of miles away, and he doesn't have family in town. The good news is that his church is rallying around him, and they're preparing a home for him to stay in after he gets out of the hospital."

"That's good. His church is his family now."

Roger had invited Owen to Riverside Chapel several times. Owen had visited at Christmas and on special event days, but not to the Sunday services. He preferred his own church, and that was normal. Not everyone had to go to Riverside Chapel, though everyone who attended there loved the preaching and the music.

"The rehab and therapy are probably going to take a long time." Cheyenne's voice sounded sad. "Months and months."

"We better pray for him." It was all Roger could say. He didn't want to ask her why she kept talking about Owen.

Was anything going on between Cheyenne and Owen?

Roger wasn't sure if he wanted to know.

Cheyenne must have sensed some questions. "He's like a big brother to me, you know."

Ah. Okay. Big brother.

"Like I said, we should pray for him."

Cheyenne smiled.

And Roger remembered all the things that she had done for him.

In twenty years since college, he had never met a woman such as Cheyenne, who selflessly gave of her time and energy to help people—both Christians and non-believers.

Her character was impeccable. Everyone Roger knew at church liked Cheyenne. The pastor's wife could vouch for her integrity.

Where could he find another virtuous woman such as she was?

And then Roger had come along, and kissed her in his office. Had he ruined their friendship in some way?

Now he wanted to kiss her again.

Just the two of them, standing here outside her front door.

He brushed away his desire. In spite of his self-imposed no-dating decade, there had always been a need in him, bubbling under the surface.

No.

No more kissing.

Cheyenne was not that kind of woman.

Roger recalled what Cheyenne had said minutes earlier

I would invite you inside, but I live alone, and I don't think it's a good idea for us to be behind closed doors, just the two of us.

Roger gulped. "I need to apologize for something."

"What?"

"The other day, in my office..."

"I remember." Cheyenne's voice was low and soft.

She knows what I'm referring to.

"I shouldn't have kissed you," Roger whispered.

"I consented. I've wanted..." She quietened.

"Wanted what?"

"Nothing you need to worry about." Cheyenne stepped back. "Oh, I'll explain to the landlady later. Come on in."

"God is our witness," Roger said as he stepped into Cheyenne's house.

It was bright and airy, considering that it was a small townhouse—the size of his upstairs walk-in closet, or maybe even smaller.

Cheyenne led him to the very small living room with one loveseat on it.

"Just overlook my mess," Cheyenne said. "The carpet got vacuumed a couple of weeks ago, when Leila did it."

"She did?" Roger didn't know much about their arrangement.

"Voluntarily. She didn't have to, but she cleaned up my little home. That was sweet of her, you know."

Roger nodded. It didn't matter to him whether Leila had inherited any traits of helpfulness. The DNA results wouldn't arrive for another week.

Yet, it mattered to him that Cheyenne had been helpful in his latest problem.

He had sent Cheyenne the flowers to thank her for her help. Well, he had meant the flowers to say more than a simple *thank you*. He had hoped to have an opportunity to speak to her in person about all that she had done for him. That had taken a backseat when Priyanka got sick on Monday, and he had to fly out Monday night to Memphis for the conference in her place.

"Would you like something to drink?" Cheyenne asked.

"Says the one-arm firefighter?" Roger chuckled.

"Make fun of my misery, why don't you?"

"I didn't mean it that way." Roger squeezed his eyes shut. He felt tired. "Oh boy."

"I have water and apple juice," Cheyenne said.

"Water is fine, but please tell me where to get it. You sit down."

Cheyenne laughed. "And here I thought Owen was the pushy one."

"Is that a good compliment or bad?" Roger followed Cheyenne into her small kitchen.

She pointed to the cabinet. Roger found two glasses and filled them with cold water from the refrigerator.

As they were drinking the water, Roger had a thought. "Have you eaten dinner?"

Cheyenne sighed. "No, but I don't feel like going out. I'm on pain meds, and I just need to rest my arm."

Roger nodded. "How about I call for a takeout? Anywhere you want."

"Anywhere?" Cheyenne stared at him.

"Anywhere in town, of course. My treat."

"I guess I could have something from Piper's."

"Others might think you'd want dinner from a five-star restaurant, but I know you better than that."

"You do?"

Roger suddenly realized what he had said. "Uh... I don't know if I really know you better than other people, but I do know that you like Piper's dishes."

"And you'd be right." Cheyenne placed her glass in the dishwasher.

Roger was still sipping his water. His heart had calmed down. "Thank God you're fine—except for that arm."

Cheyenne shrugged. "Owen saved my life. God is good."

"Maybe over dinner, you can tell me what happened." Roger paused. "If you want to."

"I've already talked to the news media, so it's not traumatic. Nobody died—praise the Lord!—but at the same time, we didn't catch the arsonist."

"Okay. We can add that to our prayer list." Roger fished for his phone. "Taking dinner orders now."

"Good timing. I'm famished."

"So am I." Roger looked up. "However, I'm glad we're both fine. Your arm will heal."

"But Owen..."

But Owen what?

"Why are you frowning?" Cheyenne asked.

"I'm not frowning. Am I frowning?" Roger tried not to move any facial muscles.

"You frowned a little bit."

"I did not."

"You did too. That's three times this evening. Every time I mentioned Owen, you frowned—there you go again."

"I'm not frowning. Stop distracting me. I'm taking orders. What would you like for dinner?"

Cheyenne smiled. "Don't worry about Owen."

Owen again.

Am I frowning?

CHAPTER TWENTY-SIX

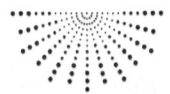

he lasagna dinner from Piper's Place hit the spot, and Cheyenne was glad that Roger stopped by her house. An hour later, they had finished dinner, and Cheyenne wanted to go to bed. Her painkiller medication was making her drowsy. She wanted to lie down to rest her broken arm.

Surely he'd understand.

She told him what painkillers the ER doctor had prescribed to her.

Roger's eyes widened. "That's a narcotic. Did they tell you to ease off it in a couple of days and use Tylenol instead?"

"Can I just switch over to Tylenol right now?"

"I suppose you can, but you might check with your doctor about it, just to be sure. I don't want you to be in pain either."

"And neither do you want me addicted to a narcotic, right?" Cheyenne smiled.

"Right."

"Well, I would have you know that I do have a high tolerance for pain, so I'm going to call my doctor in the morning and ask if I can just take Tylenol instead."

"Good move." Roger pushed back his chair. "Let me help you clean up the kitchen, and then I'll leave."

Cheyenne smiled. "When was the last time you cleaned up your kitchen yourself?"

Roger had to think for a minute. "Well, usually my housekeeper or cook does it, but from time to time, I will when they're not around—though I usually make do with paper plates or go out to eat."

"Fair enough, but I don't think it's necessary. I still have one working hand."

"I get it that you're independent," Roger said. "But I would feel bad if I leave you with dirty plates to throw out."

"I would feel bad if you stayed. Not only am I tired, but my landlady might be upset at how long you've stayed. She probably already knows I've invited you into my house—and Aunt Gemma is sure to know—and I bet she's set her timer."

"Might she have an old windup kitchen timer?" Roger chuckled.

"No, actually she has the latest iPhone."

"Does she." Roger tapped his chin with his fingers. "But your aunt already thinks we're an item."

"Are we?"

"We could be."

"But you're not for certain."

"Uh..."

Not waiting for him to form his thoughts, Cheyenne picked up her empty food container with her one working hand.

Roger took it from her. "No, no. I'll take care of it. I told you."

He waved for her to get out of the way.

Cheyenne walked past him. "Yep. You might be more pushy than Owen."

Roger frowned.

"Got you to frown." Cheyenne chuckled. "Owen. Owen. Owen."

Frown. Frown. Frown.

"I thought you two are best buddies," Cheyenne said.

"Friends, yes, but I wouldn't say we're buddy-buddy. We're not that close."

"Nevertheless, how many years have you known each other now?"

"At least ten or eleven years. Owen is my age, thereabouts."

Owen was younger than Roger, but Cheyenne didn't want to split hairs with him.

"We've already decided that when one of us marries, the other will be the best man..." Roger seemed to have more to say, but he didn't.

"I wonder which of you will be married first."

"He might, the hunk that he is."

Cheyenne didn't say a word.

She didn't think Owen was all that good-looking, but Roger seemed to think that he was at least buff.

"Don't you think that Owen looks great?" Roger asked.

Cheyenne shrugged.

And yawned.

"I better be done here and leave." Roger wiped down the small dining table, and rinsed the dishcloth.

Cheyenne waited by the counter. She added one more thing to her grocery list.

"What's that?" Roger asked, leaning to look. "Ah, a shopping list. Want me to do it for you?"

"What do you mean?"

"I'll go to the store, get everything on your list, and bring them back here. I won't even charge you for delivery."

"That's kind of you," Cheyenne said.

"After how much you have helped me with my

potential daughter, going to the grocery store is easier."

"I don't know. Each task we do has its own challenges."

"Isn't that the truth?" Roger wiped his hands. "Isn't that the awful truth?"

Cheyenne didn't answer him.

"Give me the list, please," Roger said.

"I don't need these things tonight, but I will be running out of them in a day or so. I was going to ask a friend to take me to the grocery store."

"Am I not your friend?" Roger's voice was quiet. "I'll give you a ride to the store."

"Alternatively, I could call the nearest Walmart, and they will shop for me. All you have to do is pick up the groceries at the curb."

"Then you'll miss out on the fun of selecting your own fruits and vegetables."

"That so?" Cheyenne checked her list. "With my arm in a cast?"

"I meant generally, not right now."

Cheyenne touched Roger's arm as he walked by the counter. "I'm sorry. I wasn't trying to be a difficult patient."

"I was just trying to help."

"I know," Cheyenne said. "But I can't owe you any more favors."

"No favor. I'm not expecting anything in return. In fact, I didn't three years ago."

"Almost three and a half years." Cheyenne hadn't wanted Roger to know that she had been keeping track of their friendship days—what few they had.

Now he knows.

"You counted the days?" Roger asked.

"Just the months, roughly."

"So we've known each other that long?"

Cheyenne nodded.

"And here I was thinking that I might have been too forward the other day when we...uh...we...."

Cheyenne remembered. "In your office, with the blinds up, in front of my aunt looking through the window. Who knows how long she'd been standing there."

They had a good laugh about it.

But they didn't touch each other.

"I do like you a lot," Roger said.

"People don't usually kiss just because they like each other—even if it's a lot."

Roger was silent.

Then: "Maybe I more than like you."

Cheyenne knew then that Roger hadn't figured out where she stood in his life.

"At this moment, I have a family crisis," Roger continued.

Crisis. "That's a strong word."

"It feels heavy to me. I think I can move forward once I find out if Leila a.k.a. Victorina is my daughter."

"Nothing God cannot handle, right?" Cheyenne tried to encourage him.

"I admit my faith was tested these few weeks since Leila came to town and her mother called me." Roger shook his head. "Five men. She scammed five men."

"But one of you could be Leila's real father."

"Do we know for sure? It might be someone else, one who isn't as gullible. In light of Mimi's lies, can anyone truly trust what she said about those test results?" Roger sighed so loudly that Cheyenne was startled.

She took a deep breath. "Nevertheless, in Christ we can survive this."

"We?" Roger stepped back. "This is not your burden, Cheyenne."

"Christians, especially those in the same church, do help one another," Cheyenne explained. "I'm happy to help."

"And you have done plenty. That's why I sent you flowers."

"So you don't need my help any more?"

"Probably not. Our entire goal was to get to a

conclusion. The DNA is the final chapter." His voice was quiet but firm. "So our project is over."

It seemed final.

So final.

CHAPTER TWENTY-SEVEN

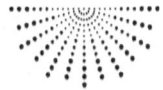

One week later, the new Sunday School teacher gave Roger a few minutes to share his thoughts with the class that he had taught for at least ten years.

It was all over now.

The good works he had done for God and church, all seemed to be negated by a secret he had swept under the couch for sixteen years, since Mimi had first informed him of a possible daughter.

The living and breathing result of a dalliance that should never have happened.

Roger's feet felt like they were encased in cement as he trudged across the carpeted floor toward the front of the packed room.

Eventually, this Sunday School class would be

too big for this meeting room, and Riverside Chapel would outgrow this riverboat.

But that was not his problem either, was it?

Roger had resigned from the church leadership committee the moment the DNA results arrived at his desk on Wednesday.

Yes, he'd had three full days to prepare this speech.

He put his stack of notes on the lectern.

Around the room, some of the class members seemed to have knowing looks on their faces. Ming and Sabine Wei, for one. Somewhere at the back, Cheyenne's face showed sympathy.

I don't need sympathy.

I need God's mercy.

Roger cleared his throat.

"When I was in medical school nineteen years ago, I met a girl in Proverbs 7:27, and I destroyed my own Christian testimony." He read the verse aloud.

> *Her house is the way to hell,*
> *Descending to the chambers of death.*

"Can you believe the Bible actually said that? I wish I had read that verse and taken it to heart before I ended up sinning against God with her. We broke up quickly after I found out that she had slept with half a dozen of my friends, if not more."

There was a bit of a rumbling in the room.

Roger glanced to the back to look for support. He thought Cheyenne mouthed *continue* to him, and so he did.

"It became a scandal when she slept with the professors as well, demanding hush money to keep the matter quiet. We—students and faculty—all broke up with her, and she left med school without finishing."

Roger turned the page. He realized that he had skipped entire paragraphs, but he didn't feel like revisiting them. "Three years later, she contacted five men—myself included—asking for DNA tests and child support. We all took the tests. And I found out later that we all matched."

"Isn't that odd?" someone in the front asked.

"Yes, it was, but we didn't know since none of us had contacted the others. Perhaps it was out of shame or something. In my case, I just wanted the whole thing to go away. However, I ended up paying child support for years. Something like ten to fourteen years."

People gasped in unison.

"One day, I found out that the other four men also paid her money. That's a lot of child support. We can't all be the little girl's father. I called everyone, and we all decided on our own to stop paying."

Roger turned the page. And again. "Ah. I'm not following my prepared statement."

He walked to the side of the lectern, looked up, and noticed his friend, Pastor Diego Flores, slip into a back row seat.

Diego nodded to him.

Thank You, Lord Jesus, for sending encouragers.

First, Cheyenne had dropped in to provide emotional and moral support.

Now, Diego came as well.

Roger felt his courage increase.

"We lost touch until last month, when the child —now eighteen—left home to find her real dad. She tracked me down, we did the tests, and lo and behold, she is my real-life daughter."

Someone raised his hand. "Did you leave out any juicy part?"

"What part?"

"You quit teaching Sunday School. You stopped filling in for Pastor Flores. Let's hear about your pit of despair."

My pit of what?

"I was not in despair. Desperation, yes. Despair, no," Roger said. "However, I can tell you that I was ashamed of my own sins. For that reason, I might have lost the woman I can truly love, all because of my shameful past."

A lady put up her hand. "Tell us about your shame, Roger."

No one laughed.

Everyone looked somber.

It was all Roger's fault that he had taught this class to be brutally honest about their own short-comings, to confront their own shortfalls, and to confess their sins before almighty God.

Now they were applying the same principle to him.

"I was about to get to that part under Lessons Learned." In the midst of his shame, Roger was quite proud of his Sunday School class. They didn't let their emotions get the better of them.

Asking him to look in the mirror in the light of God's Word was not their way of bashing him. Instead, it was their way of loving him in spite of his sins.

Not wanting to miss a lesson learned, he returned to his printed notes. He had worked long and hard on this.

Still, his hands started to shake.

Lord Jesus, please give me courage. I don't deserve it, but I need it.

After all, only God can forgive him. And He had.

Now, Roger could look back and tell his story of God's deliverance.

Across the room, Cheyenne was watching him.

I don't want to lose her...

"Go on," someone said.

Roger cleared his throat. His eyes were on Cheyenne. "I learned that redemption is more important than reputation. Sanctification is more important than shame. Peace is more important than penance."

Everyone clapped.

"You should write a memoir." Everyone laughed.

Roger felt at ease now.

Thank you, God.

"About ten years ago, I stopped dating altogether," Roger said. "I tried to punish myself for my old sins. I decided to become a lifelong bachelor, as if that would pay enough penance for what I had done, cover up my past shame, and somehow salvage my reputation."

He looked around the room. "After all, I went to med school to fix people's illnesses. I should be able to fix my own problems, right? But... What did I miss?"

A few people lifted their hands. Roger picked one.

"You tried to absolve your own sins, when the One who can forgive is God and He alone."

"Exactly. If you ask God to forgive you, He will,

and your guilt is gone—nailed to the cross of Christ. However, you may still have to deal with the fallout. A wise pastor reminded me the other day of a passage in Galatians." Roger glanced over to the back of the room where Diego was sitting.

Often, Roger had wondered whether he should stopped calling his old friend by his first name, and start addressing him as Pastor Flores. However, Diego would have none of it. They had known each other long before Diego was ordained to pastor Riverside Chapel.

"Open your Bible, if you like, as I read Galatians 6:7-8." Roger knew he had read these verses before, but he read it aloud again, as yet another reminder to himself.

> Do not be deceived, God is not mocked; for whatever a man sows, that he will also reap. For he who sows to his flesh will of the flesh reap corruption, but he who sows to the Spirit will of the Spirit reap everlasting life.

"Sin is such that there will always be consequences, big or small," Roger continued. "Say you cut off your arm. You ask God to forgive you, and He would, but you're still missing an arm. You still have to live with the disability for the rest of your life."

"God gives mercy," someone at the back said.

Cheyenne?

Roger wished that their eyes met the instant he turned toward the voice, but her eyes were somewhere else. On her lap—or the Bible on her lap. They weren't on him.

Still, Cheyenne reminded him of Leila's need for Jesus.

"My d-daughter..." He swallowed. "She's had a rough life. She's not a believer in Jesus. Cheyenne and Heidi have been trying to tell her about what Jesus Christ has done for us on the cross."

"You're a good example of the forgiveness of Christ," someone said from a seat on the side.

Ming.

Of course, one of Roger's best friends would use him as an example.

"Yes, Jesus Christ died for me," Roger said. "He also died for all of us in this room, everyone in this church, this world. And He died for my daughter. She has no hope, no salvation, no eternal life. I have to put aside my reputation, live with my shame, and consider that her soul is more important to me than keeping up my appearance as an upstanding member of our church."

Everyone nodded.

"God is good," someone said.

"Amen," Roger replied.

"Will you come back to teach Sunday School?" another person asked.

Roger didn't have to hesitate to answer that question. "Not for a while. I'll be in class, though. I'm going to sit in front, and learn more about God. Joe and Ming will do well co-teaching this class for the rest of the year. They are funny and have great stories."

"That's true," someone remarked.

Roger heard laughter and chuckles across the room, but it didn't bother him one bit.

In fact, he felt that he had gotten right with God.

And that he was finally growing spiritually, more than ever before in his entire life.

The hidden sin that had pulled him away from God was no more. In the place of it was the peace of God, enabling him to rest in Christ and learn from Him.

That mattered to him more.

All these years of hiding his secret had stunted his spiritual growth and stagnated his fellowship with Holy God.

Thank You, Jesus, for your cleansing forgiveness.

The burden—all of it—had been lifted from his shoulders.

Praise the Lord!

CHAPTER TWENTY-EIGHT

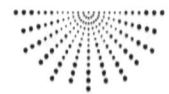

*R*oger's backyard terrace was smaller than Cheyenne had expected. Compared to the house, this terrace seemed unused. The outdoor fireplace had no logs in it. On both sides of the fireplace, a low stone wall went all around the terrace.

Beyond the wall and flagstone floor of the terrace, a boardwalk beckoned Cheyenne to go beyond the confines of the house and onto the sand and shore, to watch the sun set over the island, above the house and trees, since Tybee Island faced the Atlantic Ocean and morning sun.

I would love to see the sunrise from the beach...

The ocean waves were loud, but Cheyenne could still hear the preparation behind her, as Roger's personal chef and crew had been busy the last hour getting everything ready for this family dinner.

Family dinner?

Family?

Cheyenne wasn't sure if she could be considered family at all.

She turned around to see that Roger and Leila were coming out of the sunroom now, drinks in their hand.

Cheyenne knew that Roger didn't drink alcohol, and for that she was grateful to God. Some of her friends and colleagues drank—and she had nothing against them—but it was refreshing to see Roger stand his ground, make a statement about his beliefs.

Why did it matter, though?

Well, for someone I care about...

Cheyenne stopped herself.

Care?

What?

Roger came up to her.

"I was wondering where you went." Roger smiled. "One minute we were chatting in the sunroom, and then next I didn't see you anywhere."

"I went to the bathroom," Cheyenne said quietly. "Then I noticed that the sun was going down. I came out here to take a look."

"I see the sunrise in the mornings when I do have my breakfast here, but yeah, you have to go outside to look back to see the sunset." Roger pointed down the beach. "When I was looking for a house, they showed me one where you could see the sunset from the balcony, but it was too big for a bachelor pad."

Bachelor.

"I'm glad you could come for dinner," Roger said.

"Thank you for inviting me."

"I was afraid you'd bail out on me."

"Because?"

Roger gently touched the cast on Cheyenne's arm. "You weren't feeling too great the last time I talked to you."

"I don't like being in a cast. They put me at a desk to do paperwork. I don't know if that's me, you know, stuck at a desk." Cheyenne gasped. "Oh, I'm sorry. You work at a desk. I didn't mean..."

"Don't worry about it. I get what you're saying. You're a firefighter. You want to be out there fighting fires."

"Right."

"And I'm the opposite. I'm totally happy being at my desk at work."

"To each his or her own." Cheyenne smiled.

Roger leaned toward Cheyenne's ear. "Want to know a secret?"

"What?"

"Your arm will heal. The cast will come off."

Cheyenne laughed. "Is that what you tell the residents?"

"When they have boo-boos, yeah."

The gentle breeze around them picked up a little, pushing Cheyenne's hair across her face. She reached up to push the strands away. "I should have tied up my hair."

"I like it down," Roger said quietly.

"You're more old-fashioned than I thought."

"What? Because I said I like your hair down? I like it however you fix it."

"Good answer."

Someone called their name.

"Let's eat," Roger said, leading Cheyenne to the table.

It seemed that he wanted her to sit next to him. Like an old-fashioned gentleman—*what did I say!*—Roger pulled the chair out for her.

Cheyenne couldn't remember any of her ex-boyfriends ever doing that for her.

Leila had already seated herself next to Cheyenne and across the table from Priyanka.

Priyanka's face glowed, and she didn't look sickly anymore.

"Second trimester," she said to Leila.

From that answer, Cheyenne guessed that Leila had asked how far along Priyanka was.

"She was so sick until last week. Threw up a lot and all that." Sitting next to Priyanka, her husband put his arm around her. "But once the second trimester arrived, she bounced right back."

Must be nice to have someone you love put his arm around you like that.

Cheyenne placed her napkin on her lap with her one working arm, and reached for the full goblet of water in front of her.

Roger prayed for God to bless their food. It was a short prayer, Cheyenne thought, but she suspected that it was for Leila's benefit.

At the table, Leila was the only unbeliever. Someday, she might come around to believe in Jesus Christ as her Lord and Savior. Or she might not.

It was between her and God. All Cheyenne and the others could do was to show the love of Christ to Leila.

Cheyenne was enjoying her salad, when she heard a squeal coming from behind Leila somewhere.

She turned to look, and nearly dropped her fork.

"A family dinner!" The woman with a high-pitched voice came closer toward the dining table.

In the dusk and terrace lights, Cheyenne could see that she was wearing something that looked like a multi-colored swimsuit top, coupled with a sheer sarong and a pair of six-inch platform stilettos.

"Mom?" Leila sounded shocked. "What are you doing here?"

Mom.

Cheyenne glanced over at Roger. He looked stunned.

The woman waltzed toward Roger, planted a lightning-fast kiss on the top of his head, and then clasped her hands together. "I love family dinners. Where do I sit?"

"You're not invited," Roger said.

"I wasn't, but I am now. Bad boy, Roger, to forget the mother of your daughter. Tsk-tsk, but I forgive you." The woman waltzed around the terrace. "Look at this place! It could use a lady's touch to make it warm and sexy."

Gag.

Cheyenne wanted to leave, but she had no vehicle. Roger had driven her here and had planned on taking her home.

Even if she could borrow his car, she'd rather not drive with one arm—just in case. Maybe she could do it, though she hadn't driven with one arm before. How hard could it be?

I don't know.

But I have to get out of here.

Roger was looking at Cheyenne. His face was one of horror.

The woman returned to the table. "Wow. Priyanka is pregnant! When's the due date?"

Priyanka did not respond.

Across from her, Leila burst into tears. "Mom, leave! Please!"

"Victorina, that's not how you treat your own mother." Her voice was stern. "But I'll forgive you, since you invited me to our family dinner."

"I didn't invite you." Leila cried into her napkin.

"You told me about it."

"I—uh... You asked me what I was doing Friday night..." Leila was beside herself.

Cheyenne reached out and patted Leila on her shoulder. It was a good thing that Leila was sitting to her right.

For some reason, Cheyenne's left arm started to itch inside the cast.

The woman glared at her. "Who are you?"

"This is all my fault!" Leila was still crying.

Cheyenne wasn't sure how to reply to Leila's mother. She had just crashed a dinner party and behaved rudely.

The woman came closer, and Cheyenne smelled whiskey or some strong liquor.

Maybe she's drunk.

"Who are you?" she asked again, standing too close to Cheyenne.

You're in my personal space.

Cheyenne didn't want to give her name, and neither did she know how to explain her relationship with Roger. Was she a good friend? More than a friend?

She waited for Roger to say something.

So he did. "Ah, this is Cheyenne, one of my... uh...very best friends."

One of his best friends?

That's all I am.

Cheyenne's heart dropped. Well, it was true in many ways. They had been very good friends, and that was probably all that she could have expected from their relationship thus far.

They had done each other a favor.

Roger had rescued her from pickpockets at the Amsterdam airport some years ago.

And Cheyenne had returned the favor by helping him out with the girl who indeed had turned out to be his flesh-and-blood daughter.

The chapter was over.

In spite of the kiss in his office.

Ah, that was a mistake.

Cheyenne pushed her chair back, and got up, avoiding the woman standing between her and Leila.

"I'm sorry, everyone. I feel a bit tired and must head home." She remembered again that she had no transportation. She could call Uber or Lyft.

"We'll take you home." Priyanka saved the day.

Her husband nodded, and helped Priyanka stand up.

"Thanks, Roger, for dinner. We'll talk soon." Hunter led Priyanka around the table. "Looks like y'all have a lot to talk about."

Roger followed them through the main door to the foyer leading to the front of his house. The ladies picked up their purses from the coat closet.

"I'm so sorry," Roger said to Cheyenne.

"We'll pray for you, Cousin," Hunter said gravely.

"Thank you. I'm going to need all the prayer I can get." Roger was still looking at Cheyenne.

Priyanka gave Roger a hug.

Cheyenne didn't know what to say to Roger. She wanted to help, but this wasn't a situation she could be in. She wanted to go home and rest her arm.

"Goodbye, Roger." It was all she said.

CHAPTER TWENTY-NINE

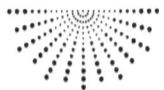

*I*n the weeks that followed that disastrous family dinner, Roger went through every work day wishing he could hide his embarrassment somewhere.

Every time he passed by Priyanka in the hallway at SSLR or ran into Miss Gemma in the dining hall, Roger remembered how Mimi Mays had messed up an otherwise nice Patel family dinner—with Cheyenne Endecott, whom he had hoped to spend more time with.

Sowing. Reaping. Sowing. Reaping.

His ex-girlfriend from medical school had persistently reminded him of his own stupidity.

And there was no hiding it.

Even if he had driven Mimi Mays out of town and out of his life.

Still, it had been too late.

In the last several weeks, Cheyenne had avoided him at church. She had left his Sunday School class to attend Heidi's new women's class.

And then last Sunday, Roger had found out from Heidi that Cheyenne wanted to visit Owen's church across town.

But why?

Hope it isn't because of me.

Monday came around again today, the start of another week of bad memories that Roger could not shake. He wondered if Cheyenne knew that he had sent Mimi away.

He wondered if Cheyenne knew that he had meant it sincerely when he had kissed her in his office in April.

And that he had deep feelings for her when he left the conference early to fly back to Savannah when she had the accident at work.

Would she put two and two together?

Roger stood at the entrance to the SSLR dining room, and realized that he had forgotten his own coffee mug, which was about four times the size of the little coffee cups in the dining room.

The smell of sausages and coffee pulled him into the dining room before he decided to return to his office to retrieve his mug.

At the breakfast bar, he ran into Priyanka, now five months pregnant.

Maybe it was a lack of sleep or something, but suddenly Roger pictured Cheyenne standing there, smiling at him, her belly bulging with child.

What would it feel like to be the father of her baby? To be there throughout the pregnancy and at the birth of their child? To raise that child together as doting parents?

What would—

"Bags under your eyes." Priyanka tilted her head. "Want to talk about it?"

Not now!

The other employees moved ahead and left the breakfast bar.

"Maybe." Roger piled up a stack of pecan pancakes on his plate. "Where's Hunter?"

"He's already eaten. Came to work two hours ago so they could start working outdoors before the sun heats up."

"Yeah. Don't want to mess with the summer heat in Georgia for sure." Roger followed Priyanka to the coffee maker, where he filled three cups with hot, black coffee, and she filled her water bottle with water.

They found a table by the window.

"This is the same table Hunter and I ate lunch at when he started working here." Priyanka settled into her chair. "I can't believe that was two years ago now."

"Seriously?" Roger wondered how much time he had to get back to Cheyenne, or whether that ship had sailed.

"Uh-huh. Time, as they say, flies like the wind."

"I don't know if it flies like the wind. You're mixing metaphors there." Roger slathered gobs of butter on his pancakes.

"Would you like to say a blessing?" Priyanka asked.

"Would you, please? I've had a hard time praying lately," Roger confessed.

Priyanka prayed.

"Amen." That much, Roger could manage.

"You know, the more difficult the circumstances, the more you should be praying," Priyanka said.

"I know."

"God has the solution to your problems, Roger."

"I know that too." Roger chewed his pancakes slowly. They were nutty and full of buttermilk. "I thought my faith was stronger than this."

"Are you asking yourself whether your faith is placed in Christ Himself or in your own Christian walk?" Priyanka chopped up the sausages into little pieces.

"Let me think about that for a minute." Roger watched Priyanka eat those little pieces of sausages.

"You know the difference."

"Yes, I do."

"You don't want to be a fair weather Christian."

"Some Christians do have easy lives. It's almost like they never have to suffer much. They get saved, they go to church, they enjoy their Christian life, they die happy, and they go to heaven."

"That's rare, Roger."

"Why can't I have that rare life?"

"Don't we all want a life of ease! We know that as we grow spiritually, the testing gets harder. If your faith depends on happy days, what weight does it have when your days turn dark and grievous?"

Roger continued eating his pancakes.

How much does my faith weigh?

"Why am I like this?" Roger asked. "I've failed God so many times. Each time He tested me, I failed."

"What are you saying? That when that woman took off her clothes in front of you nineteen years ago, it was a test from God?" Priyanka's voice sounded surprised.

"It could be."

"Well, have you considered that your own lust caused you to sin?" Priyanka logged into her phone and read James 1:13.

Let no one say when he is tempted, "I am tempted by God"; for God cannot be tempted by evil, nor does He Himself tempt anyone.

"Want me to keep reading?" Priyanka asked.

"Might as well."

And so she read James 1:14-15.

But each one is tempted when he is drawn away by his own desires and enticed. 15 Then, when desire has conceived, it gives birth to sin; and sin, when it is full-grown, brings forth death.

Roger didn't have to think about it for long. "You're right, Cousin."

Leave it to Priyanka to cut through my fog.

"Let's dissect the situation," Priyanka continued. "What do you think happened with you?"

"You mean spiritually?" Roger drank his second cup of coffee.

"I've heard a number of pastors say that every problem we have is spiritual. Even if it's an emotional issue, at the heart of it, we have a soul to deal with."

"Right." Roger ate more pancakes.

It took five pancakes for Roger to start dissecting the situation. By then, Priyanka was drinking water.

She had stopped drinking coffee since she

discovered she was pregnant. Roger could not imagine going for one day without coffee, and here was Priyanka on a coffee fast for nine months or more, assuming she would nurse her baby for a while post birth.

All the things parents do for their children.

And all he had done for Leila was pay for child support. In fact, Leila didn't even want him to pay for her college. She wanted to get there on her own. She did not want his money. All she wanted was to know that her biological father acknowledged her existence.

And thank God for working it all out.

Thank God for Cheyenne's help.

"I still think that God tested me in the situation I was in," Roger said. "I know I sinned against God. Being merciful, He gave me many opportunities to right my wrongs, but I kept ignoring them, and I kept adding to the wrongs. Sending Mimi child support payments was supposed to make things go away. It didn't. In the end, I still have to face the nineteen-year-old problem."

Priyanka nodded. "I concede you were tested."

"Thank you."

"I also agree with you that you failed miserably."

Roger laughed. "Isn't it funny? Normal Christians can sometimes behave badly when confronted with challenges."

"That's more sad than funny, to be honest."

Roger nodded. "It took me nineteen years to face my past. You know, I wondered how much I could have advanced in my Christian life if I had dealt with it when Leila was two years old."

"You thought you did. Mimi told you she was your child, the same way she told the other four men."

"The DNA test results for Leila that Mimi showed me turned out to be the real deal. She faked the copies she sent to the other four men."

"There must be some sort of federal crime for fraud," Priyanka said. "The US Postal Service will probably also investigate, since she mailed the fake results."

Roger shrugged. "I'll leave it to the other four men to deal with it."

"I'm sure they'd want their child support money back."

"I don't think Mimi can afford to pay them all back. The man she's living with is not her husband. She has three more kids at home. Apparently she couldn't hold down a job. She couldn't finish anything she started. As of five years ago, anyway."

Priyanka stopped him. "Let's focus on you. Talking about how bad Mimi is doesn't make your own sins any less bad in the eyes of God. Sin is sin. Neither you nor I can cast the first stone."

"Thank you. I need to hear that." Roger knew then that he had made the right decision to step down from teaching Sunday School. He had to get right with God before he could ever go back to teaching anyone else about God.

"I know we're supposed to start work now," Priyanka said. "But your spiritual condition is affecting your work productivity. And we're getting somewhere here. I think we need to keep talking. We can always make up for work."

"Well, I've worked so hard the last few weeks that I have at least ten or twelve hours to spare." He had been trying to forget Cheyenne, maybe, but more than likely he had been trying to distract himself from his problem.

Problem?

Most of it had been resolved.

Leila was his child. *Check.*

Mimi was gone. Roger paid her off. *Check.*

Yet...

There remained a spiritual problem.

"Do you remember last year when I had to cross my Rubicon?" Priyanka asked. "You prayed for me. Hunter prayed for me. Pastor Hiram—in glorious heaven now—prayed for me."

Roger nodded.

"I am here to pray for you. I hope you cross your own Rubicon soon."

Roger teared up. "What is my Rubicon?"

"I pray that God will show you."

"It's a lesson learned, right?"

"That's included. At the point of salvation in Jesus, you have broken free from the chains of your past. Thereafter, in stepping forward by faith in Jesus Christ, the Lord of your life, you have to grow in your faith."

"I knew that."

"Yes, but in the fog of spiritual war, perhaps you forgot."

"I might have."

"God continually sanctifies you, but if you don't learn your lesson, you cannot advance to the next step in your Christian walk with God."

"I will forever be stuck in some sort of detour, I suppose, if I don't grow spiritually."

"The question is right in front of us. What does God want you to do right now?"

"Pray?" Roger had told Priyanka that he had difficulty praying lately.

"More than that."

"Seek God? Study His Word?" Roger had been searching the Scripture, longing for God to speak to him again.

"And more. What does God require of you?"

Good question.

What does God require of me?

CHAPTER THIRTY

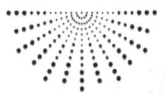

*B*y the time Cheyenne reached Piper's Place, Roger had been waiting for her at least fifteen minutes. Fortunately, he could wait at their reserved table, and not outside, where it was warm and muggy this Thursday night.

Roger's eyes lit up when he saw her. He pointed to her left arm. "Your cast is gone."

"Yes, thank God. I had to wear it for almost two months." Cheyenne placed her purse at the far end of her seat at the booth, and sat down across the table from Roger.

"I was wondering how you'd get here," he said.

"I would have called Uber."

"Of course, but I could have picked you up for free."

"That crossed my mind."

"It did?"

Cheyenne reached for the menu. "I'm sorry I'm late."

"Not a problem. I'm glad you came at all. I wasn't sure if you'd want to see me, considering you're visiting another church and all. I hope that's not because of me."

Cheyenne made a face. "When was the last time you talked this much?"

Roger sipped water. "I guess I'm nervous."

"About what?"

"I don't know. Maybe about us?"

"What about us?" Cheyenne nodded to the server, who had appeared in front of them, seemingly desperate to take their orders.

Cheyenne didn't know what she wanted to eat tonight. She decided on something light. Wild cod with vegetables on the side. Dark leafy greens for salad. "Maybe I'll save room for dessert. I don't know."

"We could go get ice cream afterwards," Roger said. "That'll cool us down this warm June night."

When Cheyenne didn't say anything, Roger kept talking. "It's on me. But we'll go only if you want to."

"I paid for only two hours of parking." Cheyenne didn't know why she said that, although it was true.

"I'm sorry, Cheyenne." Roger's voice was low. "I'm so very sorry."

"About what?"

"I drive everyone away."

"You do?"

"I'm not good with people. My cousin Priyanka is always good with people. She can read people like books. I cannot read my own self. I'm always doing something wrong with the people I love."

Love?

Cheyenne cleared her throat.

"See? I made you uncomfortable. I can't even remember what I just said to you."

Cheyenne took a good look at Roger. He had shaved and gotten his hair trimmed, but there were bags under his eyes. It made her want to ask him whether he had been sleeping good lately.

Then again, better avoid the word *sleeping*.

"Can we reboot our conversation?" Roger asked.

"What do you mean?" Cheyenne reached for the bundled napkin on her side of the table. She unrolled it and placed the fork and spoon on the small plate the server had brought for the rolls.

"First, let's say grace." And Roger did.

Cheyenne was glad that he did not hold her hands while he prayed. She would not have been able to handle it if he had done that. Seeing him again two weeks after she had stopped attending

Riverside Chapel was already reminding her of memories she had with him.

Memories like that kiss in his office.

"Thank you for agreeing to meet with me this evening," Roger said.

"Well, my aunt insisted." It was the truth. "She said if I didn't come, she's going to lose her privileges."

"Privileges?" Roger buttered a roll.

"That's what I'm here to find out."

The server brought their salad plates.

Over salad, Roger made it clear. "All the residents at SSLR are treated equally. No one has more privileges than others."

"Aunt Gemma seems to think that you treat her as more special than the others."

"Priyanka makes everyone feel special. She picks up my slack." Roger avoided eye contact. "I'm trying to be more of a people person, but it's hard. I'd rather spend my days reading charts and administrating. I'm glad God sent Priyanka to SSLR. She's the one who makes the rounds."

Cheyenne agreed. "Aunt Gemma is taken with Priyanka. She tells me stories about Priyanka."

"Stories? Like what?"

"Like how Priyanka met her husband."

"Ah."

"It's amazing how God brings people together, don't you think?" Cheyenne asked.

"Yeah. And sometimes God puts people in our lives to test us."

Cheyenne nodded. "I've had so many tests in my life."

"Me too." Roger finished his salad. "I'm sorry my real life is not pretty. You've seen the skeletons in my closet. And yet, you still meet me for dinner tonight."

"This is not a date."

"No, no. That's not what I mean. You could have said no."

"We're still friends." Cheyenne remembered what Roger had said at the dinner at his house in May.

"I consider you more than a friend," Roger said.

"You called me one of your best friends."

"I want... Why did you help me with Leila? You went so far out of your way to return a favor."

Cheyenne wasn't sure if she wanted to be honest with Roger at this time. "To begin with, I told you before that Leila needs Jesus. Is she closer to getting saved?"

"She's still where she was when we met her, but at least she's not rejecting Jesus altogether. She does come to church with me."

"That's positive for her. Since she's newish in

town, it's nice to have a community who cares for her," Cheyenne said. "I'll keep praying for her."

"She's struggling to finish her GED so she can go to college. I hope she gets her GED soon because college starts in August. Fortunately, the college she wants to attend has rolling admissions."

"Glad I don't have that pressure anymore."

"Me too."

"Did she get work and find her own apartment?"

Roger seemed to hesitate before he answered. "Well, Heidi got her a job in the college cafeteria, as you know. She stayed at Sunrise Hill for a while, but when they found out that her dad was in town, they told her that she has to go, to free up the room for a needier homeless person."

"Okay."

Roger looked intently at her. "I'm letting her stay with me until she goes to college this August. She wants to stay in a dorm to experience college life. For now, she's staying in the guest room. What do you think about that? Is that all right with you?"

"Me? What does it have to do with me?" Cheyenne had absolutely no idea. "It's your house, not mine. She's your daughter, not mine."

"I'd like to know your opinion on it."

"I'm glad she's working on her GED, and that

she wants to go to college. What's she planning to study?"

"Restaurant management or something."

Cheyenne nodded. "At least she has a major in mind, even if she changes it later."

"Agreed."

Their main courses came, and they ate quietly for a while.

"How have you been?" Roger asked.

"I'm okay."

"I want to ask you why you started going to Owen's church, but I'll wait until you finish your dinner."

Cheyenne was almost done eating. "The cod is all right, but I should've ordered salmon."

"Next time then."

"Maybe."

Cheyenne swallowed the last bit of cod. She downed it with some cold water. "Owen has had multiple back surgeries since that awful accident."

"I've been praying for him."

"Thank you. We have all prayed for him."

"And he's getting better?"

Cheyenne nodded. "A couple in his church invited him to stay with them. Their kids are grown, and they've just retired. In fact, the husband is a deacon at their church. The wife was an RN."

"God sure provided for Owen."

"He has. Still, we didn't want to just let his church do everything. Everyone at the fire station signed up to visit Owen and encourage him, you know."

"Right."

"One thing led to another, and I ended up getting invited to attend a summer dinner theater at the church, followed by a musical performance here and a women's retreat there, and next thing you know, I've visited on two Sundays. Heidi knows about this."

"I know. I asked her where you were."

"You did? I didn't think you'd notice I wasn't at Riverside." Cheyenne decided she wouldn't ask him what he was thinking about right now that he was seeing her again for the first time after two weeks.

"Are you coming back to Riverside?" Roger asked.

"Yes. This is my church. I'll be back next Sunday."

"Oh good. I thought I drove you out of our church."

"You didn't. I don't choose my church on account of people." Cheyenne thought Roger should know that. "I make my decisions on God alone."

"I thought that—well, when my ex-girlfriend

crashed our dinner that night, you left. Your last word to me was *goodbye*."

Yes, it was. "I probably meant it at that time."

"I hated not seeing you again."

Me too.

"I want you to know that Mimi has left town."

"Does it matter to me?"

"It matters to me that you know what happened after that dinner."

Maybe so. "Go on."

"It turned out that all Mimi wanted was money. Through my lawyer, we agreed that I would pay her the rest of the child support for the last five years. That makes a total of eighteen years of support for Leila. Then Mimi signed an agreement that I owed her nothing more, and that she won't bother Leila or me ever again."

"That's sad that a mother would cause so much trouble for her child."

"And she has four more kids at home. I pray they will grow up mentally and emotionally healthy."

"Leila seems to have survived her childhood. She's polite and strong."

Roger nodded. "Thank God for that. Even in the midst of difficulties, God has been gracious to Leila."

"Indeed."

"So you can come back to Riverside Chapel now, right?"

What is he thinking, truly?

Roger seemed to be waiting for her to say something.

"Roger, please understand. I went to Owen's church for two weeks to check out some activities. Since I came to Savannah, I've only ever attended one church. I told Heidi the same thing, and she understood."

Roger seemed to want more explanation.

"It's not like Riverside is lacking or anything," Cheyenne said. "In fact, Heidi and I had a good chat about some of the things we could improve at church in the women's ministry."

"Yeah?"

Cheyenne nodded. "Things that even Owen's church doesn't have."

"Like what?"

"Like a ministry for single moms."

"Single moms?"

The phrase seemed to strike Roger. There was no need for Cheyenne to explain why that ministry might be needed at Riverside, so she did not bother to go into details.

"Still, I would like to offer you my chauffeuring service to make sure that you do come back to Riverside," Roger said instead.

Cheyenne laughed. "You shouldn't pay people to go to church."

"I don't want to not see you at Riverside."

"What if it's not God's will for me to attend Riverside?" Cheyenne asked.

Roger didn't seem happy to hear that question.

"Shouldn't our answer be to go with God's will, whatever it might be?"

Roger sighed. He blinked a few times.

"You're not crying, are you?" Cheyenne asked.

"Oh no. It's dusty in here."

"Is it?" Cheyenne pushed away her plate.

The server came and cleared their table. "Would you like some desserts?"

Cheyenne looked at Roger. "I think we're going to take a walk after this, so no desserts for now. Thanks."

Roger managed a slight smile.

CHAPTER THIRTY-ONE

*A*fter walking three blocks to Cheyenne's car to put more money in the meter for the next couple of hours, it was almost nine o'clock in the evening on River Street. Roger didn't ask why Cheyenne didn't get an annual parking pass like he did.

"Remember the last time we were on this sidewalk?" Roger asked as they crossed a street, busy even at this time of night.

He thanked God that Cheyenne had come for a walk with him. Once again, she went beyond what was called for. He still wasn't sure what Cheyenne was feeling as far as he was concerned, but he didn't want to stir the waters by asking her to share her true feelings about their relationship.

"You helped me pick out a tee shirt for my

aunt." Cheyenne said. "Yellow was a good choice. She loves it."

"I've seen her wear it a few times now. She blends right in with the daffodils."

They slowed down in front of souvenir shops.

"Want to look inside?" Roger asked.

"If you want to. I don't have anything to buy, though. We're just strolling up and down River Street, aren't we?"

Cheyenne's hair was still down, and he liked it that way—although now that her hair covered her face, he wished she had tied it up.

"I don't have anything to buy either," Roger said. "Are you up for some desserts?"

"Not really. I'm sort of full. I think I might pick up a cupcake from Piper's on my way back to the car."

Roger took a deep breath. "Do you still want to walk?"

"Yes." Cheyenne smiled to him. "Why do you ask?"

"Because we're not going into stores, and we're not buying anything."

"Is that a bad thing?"

"I guess not. Saving money is good."

Cheyenne stepped closer to Roger as they kept walking. "I like walking with you."

"I could have paid for dinner."

"No, we agreed to pay on our own so it didn't look like a date."

"I know. We're trying to be proper and all. It wasn't like you didn't already know what was on my mind." Was that too much to say?

Cheyenne stopped. "What's on your mind?"

"Ah..." Seriously, he wished he hadn't said what he had said. He wished he had thought about it, and formed his words properly.

Was it premature to share his thoughts?

"We've known each other for almost four years now," Cheyenne said. "After we met in Amsterdam, we kept in touch for a whole year, before my aunt and I moved to Savannah."

"Right. And we've been friends ever since."

"We've encouraged each other whenever the other is down. When I broke up with my boyfriends or had a bad dating problem, you were always there to help me through, pray for me, and listen to me."

"Owen does that too." Roger wished he hadn't brought up Owen's name. "It might be his fault your boyfriends didn't last, although I'm glad they all went away."

"You're glad?"

"Absolutely." *Might as well tell her the truth.*

"Just so you know, Owen is more of a big brother to me," Cheyenne said. "In fact, when I broke up with my last boyfriend, Owen called you.

He didn't show up himself at the restaurant. Do you know why?"

Roger shook his head.

"Because he was pursuing a girl in his church, and he didn't want her to get the wrong idea."

"Owen has a girlfriend?"

"Not yet, but at that time, he was getting close to asking that particular girl out." Cheyenne smiled. "He's been after her for at least a year."

"Oh."

"Ironically, now that he's in a wheelchair, he is no longer pursuing her."

"Why?"

"Because he doesn't want her to respond out of pity."

"It's a male thing," Roger said.

"Is it? Or is it just pride?"

"Pride too." As he stood there outside a shop with Cheyenne, Roger wondered if he should suggest they keep walking.

The crowd was thickening. People coming out of restaurants filled the sidewalk.

"Would you like to walk along the river?" Roger asked. "It'll still be crowded there, but since we're not shopping or eating anymore tonight..."

"Who says we're not eating any more?" Cheyenne laughed. "Yes, of course, let's go."

They crossed the cobblestone road and stepped

down to the waterfront. They passed by some street musicians playing pop music from the eighties and nineties, and found their way to the edge of the water.

"My baggage is heavy." Roger had to tell her. "My burden is tremendous, but God gives me mercy and grace."

"God is good," Cheyenne said.

"In the chaos of my sin and sorrow, God gives me love."

"God is love."

Roger laughed. "Are we doing a choral reading or what?"

"It sounded like poetry."

Roger reached for Cheyenne's hand. "That's one of the many things I like about you, Cheyenne. You don't forget God and the beauty of His holiness."

"There's a verse in Psalm for that."

"Psalm is poetry and lyrics, for the most part."

"Indeed. Want me to look it up?" Cheyenne asked, already reaching for her purse.

"Sure." Why not? His only regret was to see Cheyenne let go of his hand in order to swipe her phone.

He waited for her to find the verse and read it aloud. It turned out to be Psalm 29:2.

Give unto the Lord the glory due to His name;
  Worship the Lord in the beauty of holiness.

"Beautiful." Roger wanted to hold her again again, but he felt something on his face.

He looked up, praying it wasn't a bird flying by.

In the light of the street lamps, he saw a spray of rain.

"Bummer. Looks like it's starting to rain," he said.

Cheyenne put her palm upward to test the air. "It's just a little bit of rain, but I don't have my umbrella."

"I don't either. I didn't think it was going to rain." Roger was so looking forward to this evening walk with Cheyenne.

"Well, the weather report said ten percent, but most of the time it doesn't happen, right?"

"It only rains when we don't have our umbrellas. What do you want to do now?"

"We should go home," Cheyenne said. "Hopefully we can make it to our vehicles without getting too wet."

"If we need to buy an umbrella, that might be an option too."

"Umbrellas? It's going to cost a fortune to buy an umbrella from a tourist shop."

"Yeah." She was right. "Maybe we could just

walk fast. I want to get you to your car first. I don't want you to walk by yourself at night."

"There are many people here. Police presence also. I think I can take care of myself."

"Please let me walk you to your car."

"So you do care." Cheyenne smiled as they made their way up to the cobblestone street.

"I always care."

"I know. You were always there for me."

"Through all your many breakups."

"Not many!" Cheyenne swatted his arm. "I've only had two boyfriends in four years. I've had numerous date nights, yes, but that's all because Owen was trying to set me up with his friends from his church."

Friends from Owen's church?

Roger almost froze in the middle of the street. He held his breath until they had crossed to the other side of the road.

"The same church you visited for two weeks?" Roger asked.

"Uh-huh. Why?"

"Did you see all those guys who didn't work out?"

"Uh-huh."

"And?"

"And what?" Cheyenne's voice seemed amused.

"I mean, you went to a church where you saw eligible men whom you had dated."

"Not many, Roger. Calm down."

Roger took a deep breath as they walked briskly up a road. The rain came and went. He didn't think it was necessary to buy an umbrella if they could keep their pace, but now he was having difficulty breathing for some reason.

"Do you know who remained, after all those free meals?" Cheyenne asked.

They were still holding hands.

"Who?" Roger did not want to name Owen again. No need to plant any thoughts in Cheyenne's mind.

"You."

"Me?" Roger's heart did a number on him. He didn't know what to think. It was like his slightly overweight self felt so much lighter now.

Still, he had to keep walking. He hoped he could make it to Cheyenne's car without getting more shortness of breath.

He had walked too much tonight.

But at least he was walking with his favorite person in all the world.

Cheyenne must have noticed something. "Shall we stop for a minute to catch our breath?"

"You too?" Roger stopped immediately. "I'm usually more fit that this."

"Maybe we ate too much at dinner."

"I don't know." Maybe I was scared breathless by the possible negatives.

Scared?

Why should I be scared?

Roger leaned against the old brick wall behind him.

I John 4:18 came to his mind and he recited it aloud. He had memorized this verse many years ago.

There is no fear in love; but perfect love casts out fear, because fear involves torment. But he who fears has not been made perfect in love.

"Wow," Cheyenne said. "Did something scare you?"

"I don't want to lose you, Cheyenne. I fear that if I don't tell you how I feel, you will leave, and I will never find you again."

Above them, the rain came down.

It was too late to walk back to River Street to buy an umbrella.

Cheyenne might be thinking the same thing. She stood there, staring at him.

"You haven't lost me," Cheyenne said.

Roger peeled himself off the wall. He reached for Cheyenne's hands.

"You have seen how messy my life is," Roger

said. "I have nothing to offer you, Cheyenne, except what God gives me day by day, as I trust Him."

"I expect nothing less."

Roger thanked God, as his tears blended into the rainfall, wetting his hair, face, and clothes.

Standing in front of him, Cheyenne's hair was straightening out in the rain.

"I only wish to love you with God's love, because on my own, I'm like filthy rags." Roger was on a roll, and verses were popping into his head. "I can say with the psalmist in Psalm 22:6 that I'm a worm, and in Psalm 103:14 that I'm only dust."

> For He knows our frame;
> He remembers that we are dust.

Since the streetlights were dim, Roger could not see the full expression on Cheyenne's face.

Around them, people walked up and down the sidewalk.

Roger wasn't sure if it was safe for them to stand there and talk in the rain. "I think we better get to your car."

Cheyenne nodded, taking out her keys as they walked. "Let's take a raincheck—haha!—and talk another time."

Roger prayed that they would continue their conversation soon.

They didn't talk much until they reached her car, parallel parked at the curb.

"Let me drive you to your vehicle," Cheyenne said.

"I'm four blocks away from here. We're going to get your car seats wet."

"I don't care. As long as we're both safe, we'll be fine."

When they were seated, Cheyenne locked her car, turned on the lights, and started the engine. "Tell me where to go."

And he did.

By the time they navigated through the traffic and reached Roger's car, the rain had subsided somewhat.

However, the moment was lost. The conversation was over.

They were soaked and tired and ready to go home.

Separately.

CHAPTER THIRTY-TWO

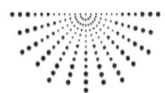

*B*oth Cheyenne and Roger had been so busy in their jobs that their conversation didn't continue for the rest of the month.

It was now July and very hot in Savannah. Aunt Gemma wanted visitors only in the mornings, right after breakfast, and before the sun baked the earth at above ninety degrees Fahrenheit.

After about ten o'clock, Aunt Gemma preferred to be inside their gathering room, where the SSLR residents would play board games, watch television, listen to music, or entertain visitors.

But first, Aunt Gemma wanted to go outside to breathe in the fresh ocean air.

For like two minutes.

Sure enough, as soon as the Georgia humidity hit her just outside the door to the courtyard and garden, Aunt Gemma waved for Cheyenne to take her back inside.

They made their way down the hallway to the connector. Beyond the glass-roof connector, the greenhouse awaited them.

Roger rarely came to the greenhouse, which reduced the chances that they would cross each other's path.

Being at SSLR offered Cheyenne opportunities to pray for him on-site.

The other day, maybe five or six days ago, Cheyenne had seen Roger briefly, just as she was leaving SSLR to go to work. He called her name first. She quickly asked how she could pray for him. He wasn't forthcoming at first, hinting that SSLR needed more funding for SLLR scholarships. When pressed, Roger confided in her that he had missed some opportunities to meet philanthropists at the conference back in April.

Since that brief meeting in the hallway, Cheyenne felt bad that she had been the reason Roger returned home early from Memphis. However, Roger assured her that he could only blame himself for not trusting God to take care of Cheyenne, for having the urgent need to see to her well-being. Cutting short his conference attendance hadn't helped anyone.

Their brief conversation affirmed to Cheyenne

that Roger had meant what he said to her on that rainy evening in downtown Savannah, when they walked to her car.

I only wish to love you with God's love, because on my own, I'm like filthy rags.

Wasn't it the best thing a Christian could ask?

Cheyenne still couldn't get over the fact that Roger had said *love* again.

Since that evening, Cheyenne had been praying for God's perfect will to prevail in their lives.

That's all I want. May God's perfect will prevail.

Cheyenne did not expect to see Roger today. He could text her if he had time. She wasn't going to make the first move.

"My new motor works well," Aunt Gemma declared.

Aunt Gemma had her wheelchair upgraded the week before, but she had told her friends that the motor had been replaced. In a way, that was true. They had replaced her motor—and the entire wheelchair.

"Is the seat more comfortable?" Cheyenne asked.

"Yes. I think it goes faster too." To prove it, Aunt Gemma pressed down hard on her remote control.

"No speeding, Aunt Gemma!" Cheyenne said even though she was sure the wheelchair went no faster than the previous one. Still, she didn't counter her aunt.

Cheyenne had to choose her battles.

Was it worth her time to fight with an elderly lady about her new wheelchair speed? Let her have her enjoyment. Cheyenne had no time to test the wheelchair or look it up on the manufacturer's website to see whether this model was faster than the other model.

They made their way to the koi pond, where Aunt Gemma was sure the koi had new babies.

Was it true or not?

Cheyenne could ask one of the greenhouse workers if she saw anyone. But again, did she want to get into an argument with Aunt Gemma? SSLR was the rest of her life for her. Sometimes Aunt Gemma was more imaginative than the average eighty-something retiree.

But let her have her fun.

Cheyenne felt strongly that she did not have to correct everything that came out of Aunt Gemma's mouth. She has a friend who spent years correcting her mother every single day in just about anything her mother did, all the way to her mother's deathbed. At the end of life, her mother said that she wished she could have heard pleasant words from her daughter.

Pleasant words are like a honeycomb,

   Sweetness to the soul and health to the bones.

To Cheyenne, the converse of Proverbs 16:24 was also true.

Unpleasant words would be unhealthy to the bones.

Cheyenne wasn't lying when she did not correct Aunt Gemma about her wheelchair speed, or whether there were new baby koi fish in the pond. In both cases, she could have researched or asked someone, and gotten the correct information to give to Aunt Gemma.

Perhaps I'll do that.

Yes, I will.

Cheyenne made a mental note to be kind if Aunt Gemma had been wrong about these things.

Still staring at the fish, Cheyenne had no idea that someone was standing behind them, until a tap on her shoulder made her turn around.

Roger.

"Surprised to see you," Cheyenne said.

"I'm sorry I have to run, but I want to give you this." Roger pressed a small card into her hand.

"What's this?" Cheyenne felt the card. It was flat.

Roger leaned toward her ear and whispered, "To go with the flowers."

"What?" Aunt Gemma raised her voice. "Say that again?"

Roger didn't. He had whispered in Cheyenne's ear for a reason.

"I have to run to a meeting." Roger waved to Aunt Gemma. "Don't fall into the pond."

Aunt Gemma laughed. "He's funny."

Cheyenne's mind was on the card, which she put into her crossbody purse.

To go with the flowers.

What flowers?

Maybe she'd find out after lunch when she went to work at the fire station.

Ah.

It dawned on her now.

The flowers that Roger had sent to the fire station a while back, the one without a message.

She smiled.

"Do you like him, Cheyenne?" Aunt Gemma asked as she wheeled herself away from the pond.

"Me?"

"Is there anyone else walking with us?"

"Uh, I guess not."

"Then it's you I'm asking. Do you like him?"

Like?

Love would be more precise.

And that was all there was to it. Beyond that, Cheyenne would leave it to God, who had made both of them. If God willed for them to be together, nothing and no one could separate them.

No one could separate them.

She recalled a verse that had been recited at weddings for centuries. A quick search on her Bible app took her to Matthew 19:6 on her phone.

So then, they are no longer two but one flesh. Therefore what God has joined together, let not man separate."

Someday, if Cheyenne ever married, she would want that verse read at her wedding.

Someday.

CHAPTER THIRTY-THREE

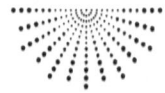

hile the card might be plain and colorless, the writing inside was anything but. Cheyenne had reread it countless times. Each time, she tried to glean clues about Roger's thought process in his words.

Would you join me for a special dinner at Piper's Place on Friday night?

Cheyenne leaned back on the loveseat and closed her eyes.

Special dinner.

That scared her just a little bit.

She stared at the card again, just in case she had misread it.

Roger's handwriting was tidy. Although it was not as neat as Cheyenne's, it was legible. He had clearly written *special dinner*.

It was a bit odd, and somewhat time-delayed. Roger had said the card went with the flowers. Cheyenne assumed he meant the flowers that he had sent to the fire station a while back, before she broke her arm. However, the content of the card was new. It was an invitation to dinner tonight.

Had Roger meant to ask her out back when he sent the flowers?

She adjusted the damp towel wrapped around her hair. She had shampooed and washed it really good. She had no time to get her hair professionally done—and she didn't want to overdo it.

Play it low key.

Feeling sweat forming on her forehead and neck, Cheyenne padded across her small living room to turn on the fan. The air-conditioner was on full blast, but she felt warm. Hot.

Fortunately, she was still in an old tee shirt and shorts, and she wouldn't drench her pretty new blouse in sweat.

Yes. I bought a new blouse to go out to dinner with Roger.

"Because of the final thing he wrote in his card," Cheyenne said aloud to no one, as she sat back down on her loveseat and picked up Roger's card again.

I have something important to ask you.

Even if it turned out to not be what Cheyenne

had suspected, it would be fine. At least she would leave dinner with a full tummy and she could keep her new blouse for another occasion.

It wasn't a fancy blouse. And it was on sale.

The iPhone on the coffee table chimed.

One-hour warning.

The clock on the wall said it was nearly five o'clock. Roger had told her that he'd be coming over at 6:15 p.m. He had been specific about it, and Cheyenne knew he would be on time, as he always had been the years she had known him.

Sometimes Cheyenne went to dinner early, way before six o'clock, but Roger had an all-important funding meeting this afternoon, and he might be running late.

On the very day he had invited her to a *special dinner*, whatever that means.

Special dinner.

What could possibly be special about dining at Piper's Place?

Cheyenne new their menu by heart. Piper changed it every spring, but for the rest of the year, the menu was pretty much the same, except for seasonal produce, and whatever bloomed in Piper's vegetable garden.

Cheyenne had checked Piper's event website. No special events today or this weekend.

It had to be some other kind of *special*.

Cheyenne recalled that Roger had handed the card to her on Tuesday, her day off. Somehow, he knew that she would be off again Friday and Saturday nights.

Someone from the fire station must have told him about her schedule this week. Cheyenne suspected that it was Owen. Although he was on medical leave, he was in contact with their colleagues at the fire station.

Cheyenne had just gotten off work several hours ago, but she was unable to nap, let alone sleep.

Between the time she got home and now, she had tried to nap several times.

All in all, she probably had no more than two hours of shuteye.

Cheyenne put the card back into its envelope, and left it on the coffee table.

She checked her phone again and yawned.

She drank some regular Coca-Cola to try to pour some caffeine into her system, before she went to her bedroom to comb her hair and get dressed.

Next to her full-length mirror, her new blouse with the pastel botanical design hung on the closet door. Somewhere in her closet, she had a pair of black pants that she wore all the time. She had laundered it two days ago and saved it for this event.

Event?

It's just a dinner.

A special dinner.

She glanced at the small alarm clock on her dresser. She had at least two alarm clocks. The battery-operated one provided her a backup to her iPhone clock—or was it the other way around?

She didn't know what happened, but it was almost 5:45 p.m.

She checked her array of sandals—all three pairs of them, all black. Should she wear this? Or that?

She wondered if she could have bought more sandals of many other colors. She had always resorted to black because it went with everything.

She wasn't trying to impress Roger.

They were only going to Piper's Place. Cheyenne had gone to that restaurant wearing sweatpants and old sneakers. No one cared what she wore.

Why does it feel different this evening?

"Lord Jesus, I'm getting nervous." Like something sweet and new was going to happen tonight.

Cheyenne took a deep breath—

And suddenly remembered that she hadn't scheduled enough time to apply makeup.

Yikes. Help me, God.

She started to sweat again.

Should I jump in the shower a second time?

She fanned her face with her hands.

After scaring herself for a minute, she calmed

down, realizing that it was only Roger Patel, after all.

They had gone to dinner countless of times in the last few years. Sometimes with Owen, sometimes with church friends, and lately on their own.

Roger had seen her with makeup, without makeup, with her hair down, with her hair up.

Never once did Roger make any funny face or remarked at how she looked.

Even if she went to dinner tonight without any makeup on, she knew she would feel comfortable with Roger.

She just knew.

CHAPTER THIRTY-FOUR

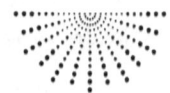

*A*s soon as Roger rang the doorbell to Cheyenne's townhouse, he quickly knelt on the doormat.

No one answered.

He inched forward on his knees, stretched his arm toward the doorbell, and pressed it twice, for good measure.

Still, no one answered.

He reached into his trouser pockets.

The one small box was still there in his left pocket.

Good.

From his right trouser pocket, he retrieved his phone. He talked to himself as he texted.

"I'm here, outside your door."

Roger scooted back to his position on the doormat.

He closed his eyes and prayed for mercy and grace and strength. "And anything else You think I might need right now, like courage and wisdom. And mercy and grace and strength."

Click. Click.

The door opened.

Standing there between the door and the doorframe, Cheyenne laughed.

Her hair was down, just like Roger liked it. She was wearing a floral blouse.

She looked tall, as he looked up from his doormat.

"What's going on?" Cheyenne asked. "Did you fall?"

"No." Roger didn't get up.

Cheyenne pointed to the tiny hole somewhere on the door. "The peephole is up here. I looked through it twice. Didn't see you."

"That explains it," Roger said.

"What are you doing on your...knees?" Her face flushed.

They stared at each other for a while.

"It's probably a bad idea to keep the door open like that," Roger said. "Mosquitoes might fly in."

Cheyenne nodded. "Would you like to come in, or is it time to go?"

Still, neither of them moved.

"Cheyenne," Roger began.

"Yes, Roger?"

"We both know that in Christ, we can do all things."

Cheyenne nodded. "Only in Christ."

"Only in Christ, can I love you with His everlasting love as a husband should love his wife..."

"Everlasting love—what?"

Cheyenne froze.

Slowly, Roger opened the small box which he had retrieved from his pocket. He took out the ring and held it on his hand.

Am I supposed to do that? I don't know.

It was too late either way. The ring was between his trembling finger now, and he hoped he didn't drop it.

The fairly decent sized diamond set in gold sparkled a little, as the last rays of sunshine swept across the front entrance of Cheyenne's house.

Perfect timing, God.

"Cheyenne," Roger said.

"Yes, Roger?" Cheyenne repeated.

"There is no other woman in this world whom I'd rather be with than you. You're the only one for me the rest of my life on earth."

Cheyenne was silent.

"I pledge to love you with the pure and holy love of God in Jesus Christ, my Lord and Savior," Roger said.

Roger could see the moisture in her eyes.

"If you say no, I understand." Roger lifted the ring toward Cheyenne. "If you say yes, it will be the answer I've been seeking for my prayers for us. You'll make me the happiest man in the world."

"I want you to be happy." Cheyenne stepped forward. "What was the question again?"

Roger frowned. "Didn't I ask?"

"No."

"Oh." He cleared his throat. "Cheyenne Colinette Endecott, will you marry me?"

Please say you will.

Cheyenne couldn't speak. She had the sniffles all of a sudden.

I was afraid of that. What if she never says yes?

Cheyenne nodded, and put her hand forward.

Roger scooted on the rough doormat, and placed the engagement ring on her ring finger. It was slightly loose, but they would resize it, of course, just as they would need to size her wedding ring.

Wedding?

He gulped, realizing the gravity of what he was doing.

But I'm sure of this.

Roger got on his feet and wrapped the sobbing Cheyenne in his arms. "I've never been surer of a decision in my life than this."

Cheyenne lifted her chin toward Roger's face.

He met her halfway with his lips. They stayed that way for a while.

Cheyenne wiped her eyes.

"I thank God for you every single day," Roger said. "You've been with me through my trials. Even when I had a difficult time spiritually, you didn't judge me. You didn't walk away. You were there, stable and strong, until I experienced the forgiveness of God in my life for my closet sins."

"I love you, Roger."

"I know you do. And I love you too." Roger smiled. "You've loved me for months, haven't you?"

"How did you know?" Cheyenne looked somewhat surprised.

"Remember that day in my office when we kissed for the first time?"

"Yeah, in front of my aunt?"

Roger laughed. "Well, you didn't protest when we kissed. I knew then that something was happening between us. That, plus all the other mess I dragged into your life made me wonder whether you'd do the same for anyone else."

"No."

"Not even for Owen?"

"What do you mean?"

"If he had a child out of wedlock, would you have helped him through the ramifications?"

Cheyenne seemed to be thinking about that question. "Well, I might pray for him, and maybe help—if I could. I mean, I signed up to help him when he broke his back—although that was because he saved my life. Why are we talking about Owen?"

"Because I was jealous of him, you know?"

"Huh. He's your friend though."

"I know, but you have no idea what I felt when you visited his church for two weeks." Roger took a deep breath. "Thank God you came back to Riverside."

"I wasn't planning on leaving."

"I thought you wanted to see what you were missing."

"I've already told you that Owen wasn't the reason I visited his church. Others have invited me too, and besides, Owen said that maybe I could help him with someone he is still interested in."

"Who? Do I know her?"

"You do. It's Officer Corazon Garcia, a friend of mine. She goes to Owen's church."

"The no nonsense Officer Garcia?" Roger had no interaction with the police officer, but he knew who she was from his friend, Ming Wei, the private investigator who had many contacts with local and federal law enforcement people, and from Camden La Salle, whose wife was almost killed in a home invasion a few years ago. Officer Garcia had been helpful to her family.

"Anyway, Cora is the liaison between the fire department and SCMPD," Cheyenne explained. "You remember the arsonist we still haven't caught?"

"I might have seen something in the news, but I wasn't paying attention too closely."

"She's been to the station a few times, and somehow she and Owen sort of hit it off."

"It can happen." Roger didn't know what else to say.

"She has asked me to attend some women's events at her church, and I've usually declined, but for Owen's sake, this time I said I would. Next thing you know, I was visiting for two weeks in a row because they had some women's luncheon after church."

"And all that's over now?" Roger prayed that Cheyenne would stay put at Riverside so they could go to church together.

"Well, for me, yes. But poor Owen. He's still trying to get Cora's attention."

"Poor Owen." Roger felt bad that he had been

jealous over nothing. The truth had now set him free. *Thank God.*

However, he still wasn't going to ask Owen to be his best man.

No way.

CHAPTER THIRTY-FIVE

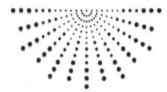

"*B*est day ever!" Aunt Gemma clapped her hands together. Her manicured pink nails with glitter accents made her gnarly fingers look at least a decade younger.

That, and her giddy behavior in the bridal room —which was basically one of the SSLR meeting rooms closest to the exit to the daffodil gardens—as she has sat with Cheyenne for a good hour or more, getting their makeup done.

Some hours before, they had gotten their hair perfectly coiffured. While Cheyenne had chosen a simple upswept hairdo, Aunt Gemma had gone all out, with jewels and gold highlights in her platinum hair.

Cheyenne glanced at her phone on the folding table in front of her to see how much time they had left before the processional would begin outdoors.

Not much time left.

She was ready, though. Her wedding gown was a simple one. Lacy, yes, but simple and modest. She had picked it out herself, with some help from her friend, Cora.

It was unfortunate that Officer Corazon Garcia could not attend her wedding today. Called out of town chasing criminals, she could not make it home in time.

Sigh.

Cora would have been her second bridesmaid.

Still, it worked out, with Aunt Gemma the only matron of honor.

"Best day ever!" Aunt Gemma repeated herself.

The wedding ceremony was to be held late morning, between board games and lunch, on this pleasant Saturday on the first weekend of April.

There was no other place Cheyenne would rather be married in than SSLR. This was where her aunt would be most comfortable, and most at home.

While it was true that the wedding day was hers, she had chosen to share it with her Aunt Gemma, who had raised her when nobody else could, who had sent her to college when she didn't need to, and who had prayed for her throughout her entire career in the US Army, and even now in her second career as a firefighter.

Aunt Gemma was always there, and so Cheyenne decided she would be here for her as well.

Roger was easy-going about it. He didn't care where they got married as long as they *did* get married.

He would have married her right away last July when he had proposed.

However, soon after the proposal and their dinner at Piper's Place, Cheyenne plunged into a busy fire season. All hands at fire stations all over Savannah were on deck chasing the arsonist—who was still at large to this day.

At the same time, the SSLR Board of Directors wanted Roger to overhaul the security of the resort and its surrounding property. They had been trying to budget for better security when Leila had walked into the facility through the side gate last year.

Not only that, Roger was also tasked to raise more funds for the SSLR scholarship. He had to take trips to meet with donors and organizations. Those trips took up a lot of his time in the last quarter of the year.

Since all that would take time to sort out, Roger and Cheyenne decided to wait.

While all that was happening, Leila earned her

GED, and was accepted by the University of Coastal Georgia to study restaurant management, of all things.

Cheyenne thought it would be best for Leila to move to the college dorms first before they repainted Roger's beach house. He wanted Cheyenne to pick out new furniture, but she would rather keep everything as it was. Their compromise was to give the walls a fresh coat of paint.

Christmas came and went, and now here they were in the first week of April, just when the daffodils were about done blooming.

"Do you like my pink shoes?" Aunt Gemma kicked up her bridesmaid gown and showed her tiny pair of shoes.

"They're very pretty," Cheyenne said.

The tiny pair of pink shoes matched Aunt Gemma's wheelchair.

Cheyenne glanced at her iPhone again. And reminded herself to leave it in this room. It would be horrifying if her phone went off during the wedding ceremony.

"I guess we're ready," Aunt Gemma said.

"We've been ready for at least an hour." Cheyenne checked off a mental list. After the outdoor ceremony, they would all adjourn to the dining room, where they'd eat lunch.

Shortly after that, she and Roger would fly out

from Savannah at 2:55 p.m. to get to Amsterdam by way of Atlanta.

Amsterdam.

Where Cheyenne first met Roger some four years ago now.

They decided they would stay in the city for a couple of days, and then take a train ride through old Europe, completing their honeymoon by rail.

Roger's brother-in-law, Hunter, would pick them up from the Savannah airport at 4:15 p.m. on a Tuesday two weeks from now.

"Are you going to be fine for two weeks while we're gone?" Cheyenne held back her tears. No point smearing her mascara all over her cheek.

Aunt Gemma reached for her hands. "Of course, I'll be fine."

Cheyenne nodded. "Make sure you eat your three meals a day, get enough naps and sleep, and exercise, okay?"

"Priyanka is going to walk with me, as she has done before."

"Very good."

Aunt Gemma smiled broadly. "I am so happy and excited for you, Cheyenne. You've grown up to be such a lovely lady."

"Thank you for raising me, Aunt Gemma."

"Your Uncle Rupert and I did it together. Team

work. God provided everything we needed and then some."

"God is good."

"Indeed, He is." Aunt Gemma tapped Cheyenne's hand. "Well, you know what God says. Until death do us part."

"Yes?"

"Rupert is gone, as you know."

"Uh-huh."

"I think..." Aunt Gemma glanced at the mirror on the folding table, and placed a finger on her cheek. "I think it's time for me to date again."

Date?

Cheyenne nearly fell out of her chair.

"You know that there are many eligible widowers at our resort." Aunt Gemma studied her pretty nail polish. "I'm going to catch the eye of a few of them this morning, I'm sure, with my pretty nails."

Oh dear. Please follow wedding protocols, Aunt Gemma.

Aunt Gemma laughed. "Look at your face."

"Ha. Whew." Cheyenne chuckled. "I thought you were serious."

"Of course, I am. Dead serious."

CHAPTER THIRTY-SIX

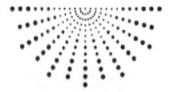

*B*aby Walden Patel-Jacobs wriggled in his mother's arms in the last seat of the second row on the groom's side. The two-month-old seemed to be quiet at the moment, but Roger watched him from where he was standing, in front of hundreds of guests, wondering what to do if the baby started crying.

You know, loudly.

In the middle of my wedding ceremony.

Well, the musicians from Riverside Chapel were playing some traditional wedding medleys. Maybe the music would drown out any baby cries. Maybe?

As if sensing his concern, Walden's mom made eye contact with Roger, and mouthed, "We'll be fine."

Or something to that effect.

Priyanka, my dear cousin.

She had delivered Walden in January, but the baby hadn't left her side at all. Every now and then, Priyanka let a babysitter take care of Walden, but only for an hour or so. She had become quite attached to her son.

Roger prayed for Priyanka that all would be well.

Her husband, Hunter, standing next to Roger, seemed to also sense Roger's concern. He leaned over to Roger. "They'll leave if Walden cries. No worries."

It would be a memory to make, since everything would be recorded.

When Roger glanced back at his cousin, Walden was not only still awake, but was spitting all over some sort of cloth that Priyanka had put over her dress.

Oh, so that cloth is for burping.

How would I know?

Roger almost laughed at his own ignorance.

Sadness threatened to creep into his thoughts. He hadn't been there for the first eighteen years of his own daughter's life. He had never changed Leila's diapers. He had never taught her to walk or ride a bike. Or taken her to a father-daughter date or dance.

Looking at how much Priyanka doted on little Walden made Roger wonder if this was what parenthood looked like.

Before he could observe more parenting skills in action, he saw that Hunter's aunt approached Priyanka. Priyanka must trust Aunt Delilah a lot, because she let her take Walden from her arms, together with that spitting cloth, or whatever it was called.

Priyanka gave Roger the thumb-up sign. Roger nodded, relieved.

He watched Aunt Delilah carry the baby—who was wriggling a lot, but not crying—all the way across the lawn, toward the meandering path that would lead to the dining hall, where the reception was to be held.

It was risky to put Leila in charge of the wedding reception. However, Leila had pleaded and begged, and her independent study instructor had agreed to advise. Leila and her restaurant management classmates had decided to start a catering business to see if they could do it at all.

Roger was the first victim—

I mean, customer.

When Leila had approached him and Cheyenne about the idea of catering their wedding reception so that she could get extra credits this semester, Roger had hoped that Cheyenne would say no.

It turned out that it didn't matter to Cheyenne either way. The only requirement she had for them was that they would work with the SSLR resident chef and food service manager, since the reception would be a luncheon.

It was not unusual for a wedding to be held at SSLR, since SSLR members themselves sometimes remarried or renewed their vows.

And there had also been many memorials over the years for SSLR members who had passed away.

Life, as they say, is short.

Stop fussing.

Nothing would remind Roger of the brevity of life more than seeing the hundred-plus residents who could make it to this patch of grass surrounded by daffodils, tulips, and other spring flowers.

Bed-ridden or sick residents could not make it outdoors this morning, but they would see the live broadcast on the television in their rooms.

For a minute or two, Roger wished that Pastor Hiram could be here. He had been such a strong counselor to everyone back when he had been alive. He had married Priyanka and Hunter two years ago.

Pastor Hiram was in heaven now, feasting with the Lord.

"You nervous?" Pastor Diego Flores asked.

"Not yet." Roger was glad that his good friend was available to officiate his wedding this Saturday. Roger would have moved the wedding date if Diego could not make it.

Diego and his wife had been happily married for many years.

Roger looked across the room to find all the other friends from Riverside Chapel who had found their best friend in life, and who were content in their marriages.

Spread among the residents of SSLR were his friends from church. Ming and Sabine, Tamsyn and Ryan, Camden and Iris.

There were other church members of Riverside Chapel who had married in the last ten years, but some had moved out of town.

In the front row were Roger's family members. His parents had flown in from Vancouver for the occasion. They sat next to Priyanka's father from India, who had come a long way to celebrate his nephew's matrimony.

His brothers, Rhett and Vijay, whom he hadn't seen in a few years due to their busy work schedules, were sitting in the same row as their parents.

Slipping in at the end of the row, Leila's hair was tied up in a bun on top of her head. She looked more and more like Roger's mother, who had been terribly surprised to find out about Roger's secret.

After not talking to him for about twenty-four hours, his mother finally called and asked to meet with her sudden granddaughter, their first in the family.

On the bride's side, Cheyenne's only family member currently alive was Miss Gemma, but God had provided co-workers and colleagues. And friends from Riverside Chapel and Sunrise Church.

Most of the seats were taken by firefighters and local law enforcement officers, friends of Cheyenne.

Somewhere to the side, Owen was chatting with his friends. Roger wondered when he might be able to walk on his own again, but there were still more surgeries to come. His girlfriend wasn't here today. Officer Garcia had been called away for work reasons.

A noise distracted Roger, and he saw the pinkest apparition on the planet.

Dressed in all pink, Miss Gemma—soon to be Aunt Gemma—was making her way up the cement path in her motorized pink wheelchair.

Cheyenne's matron of honor, Miss Gemma was all glowing.

This means it's almost time.

Time?

Almost time?

Roger's palms began to sweat.

Is the morning getting hot?

He glanced up to the sky. It was partially cloudy. No chance of rain, according to the weather forecast. The temperature would be mild. Humidity low.

His palms continued to sweat.

Maybe I'm getting sick.

The musicians changed their song to Bach's *Jesu, Joy of Man's Desiring*.

The processional song reminded Roger of Jesus Christ, the Savior of his soul and the Lord of his heart. If God had brought him and Cheyenne to this day, God would also lead them the rest of their lives until He led them home to heaven.

Roger's palms stopped sweating.

Thank You, Jesus.

And there she was.

The love of his life.

Cheyenne's face was smiling under the veil. He could see that glow on her cheeks.

Walking up the stone path toward Roger and their pastor, Cheyenne was smiling broadly under the veil.

Roger could see the glow on her cheeks even from this distance.

Her hand was in the arm of her fire chief, Captain Takayama, who had agreed to walk her down the aisle.

From his conversations with Cheyenne, Roger

knew that she had felt deeply about Uncle Rupert not being alive today. Cheyenne had decided that Captain Takayama was like an uncle to her, and he had agreed to do the honors.

Roger's eyes were on Cheyenne only, and he didn't hear the music stop and Diego speak.

Diego had to clear his throat.

"Would the bride and groom look this way, please?" Diego said in his pastor voice.

Roger realized that he was still staring at Cheyenne.

Uh-oh.

They both turned to face Diego.

Roger held Cheyenne's hand the entire time, as their pastor officiated the happiest and yet most solemn occasion.

Roger tried to keep his emotions in check. Yet the realization was clear.

I'm not worthy of her love and I will never be.

Only Christ is worthy.

Roger found it incredible that Cheyenne would take him to be her husband—along with his faults and flaws, with all his sins and sorrows.

She still wants to marry me.

"I pronounce you husband and wife," Diego said. "You may kiss the bride."

Out of the blue, someone squealed. "Kiss! Kiss!"

Cheyenne's mouth dropped, and her cheeks reddened.

Roger heard that loud voice too.

Miss—now Aunt—Gemma.

And he remembered how she had witnessed him kissing Cheyenne for the first time last year. *Has it been a year already?*

Roger lifted Cheyenne's veil, and dipped his lips toward hers.

It was a gentle kiss—fairly quick and chaste—because Roger suddenly felt shy in front of at least eighty percent of the SSLR residents, although surely they had all seen wedding kisses sometime in their lifetimes.

"Ladies and gentlemen," Diego said. "May I introduce you to Mr. and Mrs. Roger Patel."

Everyone clapped, as Roger and Cheyenne waved to their wedding guests.

Honk!

Startled, Roger's eyes widened. The honking noise came from behind them.

Honk! Honk!

Cheyenne gasped.

It can't be.

Roger spun around, as Aunt Gemma lifted up her pink bike horn and gave it another squeeze.

Honk!

The entire crowd laughed.

Horrified, Roger was too stunned to speak. Should he grab the horn from Aunt Gemma and make a scene on his own wedding day? After all, no bike horns were allowed on SSLR property.

Hadn't he confiscated all of Aunt Gemma's horns?

How many new ones had she bought to replace those taken away from her?

Honk! Honk!

"We have all these things on video," Roger whispered in Cheyenne's ear.

"Yes."

Honk!

"Memories for posterity," Roger muttered under his breath.

"It's life uncut, isn't it?" Cheyenne said.

With only a light layer of makeup, Cheyenne's face glowed in the April sun, in a natural look that made Roger stare.

And stare.

"With God, we can take it all in stride." She smiled.

Roger closed his eyes. Cheyenne was right.

God is still good, no matter what happens.

"With God, we will be fine," Roger said, believing it.

"With God, all will be well," his bride replied.

"Amen."

Honk!

~

DEAR READER:

Thank you for reading *Find You Again*. I hope you enjoyed the story of Roger and Cheyenne. The next novel after *Find You Again* is *Wish You Joy*, a Christmas-themed romance that begins in the hot summer month of July when Chrismastown starts preparing for their upcoming holiday decorating season. We will finally catch up with the Untermeyer family and see what other secrets fall out of their closet.

Wish You Joy (Savannah Sweethearts Book 10)
JanThompson.com/wish

READ A FREE EBOOK!

Set in Georgia, South Carolina, and Tennessee, this Christian romance tells the story of art gallery archivist Sheryl Breckenridge and world-famous sculptor Winton Pace. This prequel is in the same story world as Savannah Sweethearts.

Time for Me (A Vacation Sweethearts Prequel)

JanThompson.com/time-free

JOIN MY BOOK NEWS MAILING LIST

Want to keep up with my writing schedule and get the latest book news from me? Sign up for my mailing list and read my newsletters for behind-the-scene information as well as to get free and discounted books.

Jan Thompson's Mailing List
JanThompson.com/newsletter

PLEASE LEAVE A REVIEW

Thank you again for reading *Find You Again*. If you'd like to leave a review, please follow the link below.

Find You Again (Savannah Sweethearts Book 9)
JanThompson.com/find

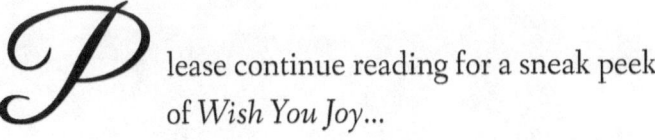lease continue reading for a sneak peek of *Wish You Joy*...

THE NEXT BOOK IS WISH YOU JOY

SAVANNAH SWEETHEARTS BOOK 10

The new CEO of Christmastown USA celebrates Christmas year round. His business partner would rather not have Christmas at all.

Christmastown USA has a new CEO. However, owning a majority share of the holiday-decorating company makes no difference for Cyrus Theroux if the other forty-nine percent refuses to cooperate...

CYRUS'S CHRISTMAS...

Whoopee! Christmastime is here again.

Cyrus is so excited that he is beside himself. Never mind that it's ninety-three degrees outside in the middle of a hot July in Savannah. Christmas will be here any day now. He has checked his Christmastown USA warehouse twice, counted his inventory four times, and added ten new team members to join his thirty. He can spread them all over town. Sure, he can manage the decorating teams himself, even if his business partner can't handle it.

What's with Amy Untermeyer anyway? Maybe he should consider buying her share of the company. He will keep Mr. Untermeyer's memories and wishes alive. Yes, that's what he'll do. Kick Amy off the sleigh and keep Christmastown all to himself—

No.

There was something about Amy that draws Cyrus to her. Something he can't put his thumb on...

AMY'S ANGST...

Christmas is too commercialized!

Amy simply cannot believe how anyone could focus on the Christ of Christmas when people over-spend and get stressed out at festivities they cannot enjoy with family members and relatives they do not wish to see or buy presents for.

Why Mom has given Amy a forty-nine percent share of Christmastown USA, she'll never know. Amy doesn't want it, but she can't sell it. To sell her share to some stranger would disrespect the memory of Dad, who inherited this business from Grandpa Earnest, who had started the company back in the fifties. The entire Untermeyer family lives from Christmas to Christmas. It was because of Christmastown that Amy's parents were able to send her and her two brothers to college.

Amy cherishes the happy memories of her child-hood and the Untermeyer legacy until some devas-tating news makes her question everything she has ever known about the Untermeyer family...

A Christmas theme holiday romance, *Wish You Joy* is Book 10 in *USA Today* bestselling author Jan Thompson's **Savannah Sweethearts** series of sweet, clean, wholesome, and inspirational multiethnic contemporary Christian romances celebrating faith, hope, and love in Jesus Christ.

Continue reading for a sneak peek of *Wish You Joy* Chapter 1...

"Let me get this straight." Cyrus Theroux splayed his fingers on the long worktable at one corner of the warehouse.

He glared at Mrs. Untermeyer's daughter, sitting

across the table from him. Her back was facing the exit sign leading to the lobby and lunchroom. Above them, the high ceiling of the cavernous warehouse loomed, waiting for the other shoe to drop.

Cyrus drew a deep breath, forming his next words cautiously. "I told you that Christmastown operates on a five-year business plan, but you just said you have no idea what you'll be doing in five months."

"I'm a destination wedding photographer, and I go where I get paid," Amy Untermeyer said.

"But five months from now, we're smack dab in the middle of Christmas."

Amy shrugged.

"It sounds—and looks—like you don't care about the company your grandpa started." Cyrus frowned as best he could to emphasize his point.

Well, maybe he shouldn't have played the emotion card, but the words had left his lips.

Amy remained seated. "I care, but Mom was supposed to run it, keep it in the family."

"In case you haven't noticed, your mother is up there in age, and she's got a bad hip and a couple of bad knees. She's been talking about moving to an assisted-living home."

Amy looked stunned, like that was new information to her.

Cyrus wondered if he should have said all that, but there it was. Those words had rolled out onto the battlefield and now faced this Goliath.

Amy looked like she didn't know how to respond.

Usually, Cyrus could read faces pretty well, but this time, he couldn't figure out which way the conversation was going, so he waited for Amy to make the next move.

She sat there. Stoic. Silent.

"Your mother said that her sons approved," Cyrus added.

Well, okay, bringing in Amy's brothers—one deployed in the Special Forces to places unknown, the other a chef on a cruise ship somewhere, and both who hadn't come home for Christmas in a few years—probably was a bad idea.

"My brothers?" Amy chuckled. "They don't care about Christmastown."

"And you do?"

Ouch. Cyrus quickly prayed for wisdom from God to shut his mouth *before* he snapped out another snide remark.

Still, it was true. Mrs. Untermeyer had said that while she had seen her sons once three years ago, this was the first time Amy had come home for a visit in five years. The fact that she was only here for a couple of days would make nary a difference in his business plan.

"Mrs. U sold me fifty-one percent of Christmastown last year. I've been running the company all this time, and we've been doing well. And now you show up." Cyrus straightened up. "You're dropping in for an inspection?"

"I was out of the country last Christmas, and I let it go. I thought I had time to discuss things with you. When Dad was running Christmastown, he didn't open for business until October. I didn't expect the warehouse to be operational in the summer."

"Well, this is how I run things, Miss Untermeyer. I'm growing the company, and it's open year around." Just for good measure, Cyrus repeated it. "All. Year. Round."

"It's still July!" Amy said. "Christmas doesn't begin in July. It doesn't even begin until after Thanksgiving."

"Says who? Some people put up a tree at the end of October."

"You do?" Amy asked.

"Aunt Marie wants it up by early November."

And Cyrus's uncle, Melvin Theroux, would do it for her sake, year after year. But this year, Uncle Mel was beginning to become as feeble as Aunt Marie.

Amy's face finally changed. "How's Marie?"

"She just turned eighty-six years old."

"No way."

"Uncle Mel is pushing ninety-five. Can you believe it?"

"Well, he'd always looked wrinkly...pardon me."

Cyrus laughed. "Aunt Marie sometimes calls him her shar-pei. Woof!"

"Might be because he's out in the sun a lot in that nursery of his. Does he still have it?"

"He sold it to me." Cyrus stopped laughing. "And that's how it all began. Mrs. U was at the nursery, ordering poinsettias for Christmastown, when I was getting a tour of the tree farm next door."

Amy said nothing.

Cyrus wondered what was going through her mind. He wished he hadn't mentioned the tree farm.

He had wanted the Christmas tree farm as part of the sale of Christmastown, but Mrs. Untermeyer had held it back. Said her husband would have wanted her to keep maintaining it.

Cyrus would be more than happy to take over the tree farm.

It dawned on him that if Mrs. Untermeyer gave Amy the tree farm, his prickly business partner would suddenly have at least 55 percent of the shares of Christmastown.

Yikes.

Time to put my guard up!

The last thing he needed was to let Amy have leverage. He wanted to run Christmastown the way he wanted to run it. So there.

He studied the woman across the table. She still showed no emotions, except for that shrug earlier and her stunned look a bit later. He wondered how much he should say, and decided to summarize it, just in case she had some nefarious motives up her sleeves to reclaim or take over Christmastown.

There was no way he was going to let this world-traveling absentee daughter of Mrs. Untermeyer's snatch this proper business out of his hands.

"So in one fell swoop, you bought two businesses," Amy finally said.

"Struggling businesses. I could lose all my money." In retrospect, he shouldn't have sold his house in Atlanta, some stocks, and all of his inheritance money to pay for them.

He had done what he hadn't learned at the MBA program at Clemson: put all his eggs into one basket.

Sometimes Cyrus wondered if Mrs. Untermeyer's whole reason of shaking up her family business was to bring her only daughter home to Savannah.

Well, here she is.

Pretty she might be, but roses have thorns...

"Look, I need this company to thrive," Cyrus said. "Or else I've lost all my investment."

"That's the problem. The love of money is the main reason gobs of companies have cannibalized Christmas!"

"You mean commercialized Christmas?"

"I said *cannibalized*. Did you want to speak for me?"

"Ah... No, ma'am. Sorry. Go on." Cyrus felt slapped. Just because Amy looked like she was still in her twenties—at most, late twenties—compared to his early thirties, it didn't mean he could look down on her as being still a youth.

"Like I said, Christmas doesn't begin in July," Amy snapped. "Do you know it's ninety-three degrees outside today?"

Cyrus wanted to say something, but Amy waved her arms about.

He didn't have to turn around to know that she was pointing to the interior of the warehouse behind him, to the rows of shelves and boxes, the forklifts passing by them with more shipment from China. Fake Christmas trees that they could store year round.

"All these represent the cannibalization of Christmas," Amy said above the noise of the passing forklift.

"Didn't your dad build this warehouse to replace an old one?"

"Yeah, but Christmas wasn't this commercialized when I was growing up."

"We all long for days gone by," Cyrus hissed.

"All? Not all."

"Are you correcting my words now? Speaking for me?" Cyrus tipped his head.

"Touché."

"We make a great pair—uh... Why did I say that?" Cyrus leaned back in his chair.

"They're just words." Amy seemed to brush him off. "The point is, Jesus wasn't even born in December, was He? Christmas is a commemorative season, not a real birthday holiday."

"I, for one, am glad we have a time of year to remember Jesus, who is my personal Lord and Savior. We have Christmas, and we have Easter."

"Don't get me started on Easter. Some say the word is derived from an old word for some spring goddess. Does that sound biblical to you?"

Yikes. Where is this woman from? "Don't you think we need to celebrate the death, burial, and resurrection of Jesus Christ?"

"Yes, but why don't we call it Resurrection Sunday instead of Easter Sunday?"

"We can," Cyrus said. "Others might not want to. It's their prerogative. But back to Christmas.

Christmastown is a decorating business, and that has been the focus since your grandpa started the company back in the fifties, according to Mrs. U."

Now Amy was visibly moved.

Maybe it was because Cyrus had mentioned Grandpa Earnest. He wanted to test it again, but he'd better not. No point poking the rattlesnake when she was already riled up.

But it was time for him to end the meeting and get back to business.

"Miss Untermeyer, if you feel that strongly about un-Christmas, feel free to sell me your *minority* share of Christmastown," he said.

"Why should I? The memory of my dad is in Christmastown." Amy's shoulders slacked. She sank into the chair. Pointed here and there. "I used to come here with my brothers, and we'd skate up and down those aisles. Dad would be furious when he found us."

Cyrus turned his head to see where Amy was pointing. "It's dangerous to play in a working warehouse."

"We were teens."

"Yeah. I've been a stupid—strike that!—regular teen myself." Cyrus cleared his throat.

"You said it. I didn't. I was the one who always got into trouble with...with..."

Silence.

"Grandpa Earnest?" Cyrus took in a deep breath. "Tell you what. We just met each other when you walked in an hour ago. Let's just take it easy, and talk business another time."

"There's no other time. I'm gone in two days, remember?"

"When you come back then?"

"After Christmas."

"Wow." Cyrus prayed quickly for the right words. "You're not coming home for Thanksgiving and Christmas again?"

"Home? Savannah is Mom's hometown, not mine..."

Even as her words trailed off, Cyrus sensed some sort of nostalgia. And remorse, perhaps?

Amy sighed. "After Christmas I have some weddings to shoot in Auckland, then Rio."

"Auckland, as in New Zealand? Rio, as in Brazil?"

Amy nodded.

"All the way to the Southern Hemisphere?"

"That's where those places are, the last time I checked. It'll be warm-weather weddings in January. Your point, Cy?"

Cy? She calls me Cy?

Nobody calls me Cy but my close friends... and Mom.

"I'm sorry. You don't like to be called Cy," Amy said.

"Huh?"

"Your face just changed."

"What?"

"When I called you Cy."

"I just had a memory. That's all."

"Memory of?"

"Mom." Cyrus didn't know why he answered her. It had been a private thought. *Oh well. It's out now.* "She called me Cy all the time."

"Called?"

"She passed away last year. She left me all her inheritance—I'm her only son—and I spent it all on Christmastown. It has to work, or I've failed big time." Cyrus straightened up. "Look, I'll be putting in a thousand percent of myself into this company, and I only have fifty-one percent of the profits. It seems to me that if you're going to leave after Christmas—or whenever—you're declaring that you're not doing your fair share."

"I have a job to get back to."

"Well, this is my job now. If you do nothing—or only one or ten percent—and I run the company all by myself when you're not here, it's hardly fair for you to get forty-nine percent of the profits."

Amy didn't reply, so Cyrus continued. "Sell me your share, and you can go free, back to your travels or whatever. I'll gladly do all the work here to keep Christmastown going."

Cyrus waited.

"You're not an Untermeyer," Amy finally said.

"And you know how to be one?"

As soon as Cyrus said those indicting words, Amy sprang up from her seat and strutted out of the noisy warehouse, leaving him sitting there, wondering what he had just done.

Wish You Joy (Savannah Sweethearts Book 10)
JanThompson.com/wish

Savannah Sweethearts:
JanThompson.com/savannah

For Savannah Sweethearts Book News:
JanThompson.com/newsletter

ACKNOWLEDGMENTS

Many thanks to my Georgia Press publishing team for keeping up with my writing schedule.

For this book, I thank my proofreader extraordinaire, Lenda Selph, whose eye for copyediting details is from the Lord.

I appreciate my early readers who kindly read this novel ahead of the world: Debbie Jamieson, Paula Marie, Julia Wilson, and Elizabeth Dent.

I am grateful to God for my husband and son for their support and encouragement. I also thank God for my parents and my three brothers for my happy and memorable childhood. I'll always remember my beloved mother and my late father for having instilled in me the love of reading and writing from a very early age. I miss my father here on earth, but I will see him again in heaven someday.

Most of all, I am eternally thankful to my Lord and Savior, Jesus Christ, who died on the cross to save me from my sins and rose again from the grave to give me eternal life. Without Him, I can write nothing (John 15:5).

Joyfully in Jesus,
Jan Thompson
John 3:16

BOOKS BY JAN THOMPSON

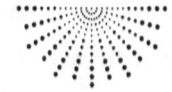

CONTEMPORARY CHRISTIAN ROMANCE:
CITY, COASTAL, AND BEACH

Seaside Chapel (7 Books)
JanThompson.com/seaside
Savannah Sweethearts (12 Books)
JanThompson.com/savannah
Vacation Sweethearts (8 Books)
JanThompson.com/vacation
Midtown Christmas (4 Books)
JanThompson.com/christmas

CHRISTIAN ROMANTIC SUSPENSE AND
NEAR-FUTURE TECHNOTHRILLERS

Protector Sweethearts (6 Books)
JanThompson.com/protector
Defender Sweethearts (6 Books)
JanThompson.com/defender
Binary Hackers (4 Books)
JanThompson.com/binary

Subscribe to Jan Thompson's mailing list:
JanThompson.com/newsletter

ABOUT JAN THOMPSON

USA Today bestselling author Jan Thompson writes clean and wholesome contemporary Christian romance with elements of women's fiction, Christian romantic suspense with an air of mystery, and inspirational international thrillers with threads of sweet Christian romance. Jan's books are for readers who love inspiring stories of faith, hope, and love in Jesus Christ.

Raised on a tropical island in the eastern hemisphere, Jan now lives and writes in the western hemisphere. Her international background gives her a unique multicultural and multiracial perspective to her novels and books. The island has never left her, and she reminisces about beach life in her beach romance novels.

When Jan is not busy writing small-town stories, she writes big-city romantic suspense and international technothrillers, a nod to her previous career in computer science. She weaves technology with human interests, reflecting the current and future digital world. And romance. There's always romance.

Beyond the printed page, Jan is a wife, mother, family scribe, avid reader, occasional artist, erstwhile pianist, and chief of staff to the family cat.

Find out more about Jan Thompson:
JanThompson.com

Subscribe to Jan's book news mailing list:
JanThompson.com/newsletter

For God so loved the world,
that He gave His only begotten Son,
that whosoever believeth in Him should not perish,
but have everlasting life.

—John 3:16